Cousin Phillis

by Elizabeth Gaskell

Wilder Publications, LLC.
PO Box 3005
Radford VA 24143-3005

ISBN 10: 1-60459-466-7
ISBN 13: 978-1-60459-466-9

Cousin Phillis

Part I

It is a great thing for a lad when he is first turned into the independence of lodgings. I do not think I ever was so satisfied and proud in my life as when, at seventeen, I sate down in a little three-cornered room above a pastry-cook's shop in the county town of Eltham. My father had left me that afternoon, after delivering himself of a few plain precepts, strongly expressed, for my guidance in the new course of life on which I was entering. I was to be a clerk under the engineer who had undertaken to make the little branch line from Eltham to Hornby. My father had got me this situation, which was in a position rather above his own in life; or perhaps I should say, above the station in which he was born and bred; for he was raising himself every year in men's consideration and respect. He was a mechanic by trade, but he had some inventive genius, and a great deal of perseverance, and had devised several valuable improvements in railway machinery. He did not do this for profit, though, as was reasonable, what came in the natural course of things was acceptable; he worked out his ideas, because, as he said, 'until he could put them into shape, they plagued him by night and by day.' But this is enough about my dear father; it is a good thing for a country where there are many like him. He was a sturdy Independent by descent and conviction; and this it was, I believe, which made him place me in the lodgings at the pastry-cook's. The shop was kept by the two sisters of our minister at home; and this was considered as a sort of safeguard to my morals, when I was turned loose upon the temptations of the county town, with a salary of thirty pounds a year.

My father had given up two precious days, and put on his Sunday clothes, in order to bring me to Eltham, and accompany me first to the office, to introduce me to my new master (who was under some obligations to my father for a suggestion), and next to take me to call on the Independent minister of the little congregation at Eltham. And then he left me; and though sorry to part with him, I now began to taste with relish the pleasure of being my own master. I unpacked the hamper that my mother had provided me with, and smelt the pots of preserve with all the delight of a possessor who might break into their contents at any time he pleased. I handled and weighed in my fancy the home-cured ham, which seemed to promise me interminable feasts; and, above all, there was the fine savour of knowing that I might eat of these dainties when I liked, at my sole will, not dependent on the pleasure of any one else, however indulgent. I stowed my eatables away in the little corner cupboard–that room was all corners, and everything was placed in a corner, the fire-place, the window, the cupboard; I myself seemed to be the only thing in the middle, and there was hardly room for me. The table was made of a folding leaf under the window, and the window looked out upon the market-place; so the studies for the prosecution of which my father had brought himself to pay extra for a sitting-room for me, ran a considerable chance of being diverted from books to men and women. I was to have my meals with the two elderly Miss Dawsons in the little parlour behind the three-cornered shop downstairs; my breakfasts and dinners at least, for, as my hours in an evening were likely to be uncertain, my tea or supper was to be an independent meal.

Then, after this pride and satisfaction, came a sense of desolation. I had never been from home before, and I was an only child; and though my father's spoken maxim had been, 'Spare the rod, and spoil the child', yet, unconsciously, his heart had yearned after me, and his ways towards me were more tender than he knew, or would have approved of in himself could he have known. My mother, who never professed sternness, was far more severe than my father: perhaps my boyish faults annoyed her more; for I remember, now that I have written the above words, how she pleaded for me once in my riper years, when I had really offended against my father's sense of right.

But I have nothing to do with that now. It is about cousin Phillis that I am going to write, and as yet I am far enough from even saying who cousin Phillis was.

For some months after I was settled in Eltham, the new employment in which I was engaged–the new independence of my life–occupied all my thoughts. I was at my desk by eight o'clock, home to dinner at one, back at the office by two. The afternoon work was more uncertain than the morning's; it might be the same, or it might be that I had to accompany Mr Holdsworth, the managing engineer, to some point on the line between Eltham and Hornby. This I always enjoyed, because of the variety, and because of the country we traversed (which was very wild and pretty), and because I was thrown into companionship with Mr Holdsworth, who held the position of hero in my boyish mind. He was a young man of five-and-twenty or so, and was in a station above mine, both by birth and education; and he had travelled on the Continent, and wore mustachios and whiskers of a somewhat foreign fashion. I was proud of being seen with him. He was really a fine fellow in a good number of ways, and I might have fallen into much worse hands.

Every Saturday I wrote home, telling of my weekly doings–my father had insisted upon this; but there was so little variety in my life that I often found it hard work to fill a letter. On Sundays I went twice to chapel, up a dark narrow entry, to hear droning hymns, and long prayers, and a still longer sermon, preached to a small congregation, of which I was, by nearly a score of years, the youngest member. Occasionally, Mr Peters, the minister, would ask me home to tea after the second service. I dreaded the honour, for I usually sate on the edge of my chair all the evening, and answered solemn questions, put in a deep bass voice, until household prayer-time came, at eight o'clock, when Mrs Peters came in, smoothing down her apron, and the maid-of-all-work followed, and first a sermon, and then a chapter was read, and a long impromptu prayer followed, till some instinct told Mr Peters that supper-time had come, and we rose from our knees with hunger for our predominant feeling. Over supper the minister did unbend a little into one or two ponderous jokes, as if to show me that ministers were men, after all. And then at ten o'clock I went home, and enjoyed my long-repressed yawns in the three-cornered room before going to bed. Dinah and Hannah Dawson, so their names were put on the board above the shop-door–I always called them Miss Dawson and Miss Hannah–considered these visits of mine to Mr Peters as the greatest honour a young man could have; and evidently thought that if after such privileges, I did not work out my salvation, I was a sort of modern Judas Iscariot. On the contrary, they shook their heads over my intercourse with Mr Holdsworth. He had been so kind to me in many ways, that when I cut into my ham, I hovered over the thought of asking him to tea in my room, more especially as the annual fair was being held in Eltham market-place, and the sight of the booths, the merry-go-rounds, the wild-beast shows, and such country pomps, was (as I thought at seventeen) very attractive. But when I ventured to allude to my wish in even distant terms, Miss Hannah caught me up, and spoke of the sinfulness of such sights, and something about wallowing in the mire, and then vaulted into France, and spoke evil of the nation, and all who had ever set foot therein, till, seeing that her anger was concentrating itself into a point, and that that point was Mr Holdsworth, I thought it would be better to finish my breakfast, and make what haste I could out of the sound of her voice. I rather wondered afterwards to hear her and Miss Dawson counting up their weekly profits with glee, and saying that a pastry-cook's shop in the corner of the market-place, in Eltham fair week, was no such bad thing. However, I never ventured to ask Mr Holdsworth to my lodgings.

There is not much to tell about this first year of mine at Eltham. But when I was nearly nineteen, and beginning to think of whiskers on my own account, I came to know cousin Phillis, whose very existence had been unknown to me till then. Mr Holdsworth and I had been out to Heathbridge for a day, working hard. Heathbridge was near Hornby, for our line of railway was above half finished. Of course, a day's outing was a great thing to tell about in my weekly letters; and I fell to describing the country–a fault I was not often guilty of. I told my father of the bogs, all over wild myrtle and soft moss, and shaking ground over which we had to carry our line; and how Mr Holdsworth and I had gone for our mid-day meals–for we had to stay here for two days and a night–to a pretty village hard by, Heathbridge proper; and how I hoped we should often have to go there, for the shaking, uncertain ground was puzzling our engineers–one end of the line going up as soon as the other was weighted down. (I had no thought for the shareholders' interests, as may be seen; we had to make a new line on firmer ground before the junction railway was completed.) I told all this at great length, thankful to fill up my paper. By return letter, I heard that a second-cousin of my mother's was married to the Independent minister of Hornby, Ebenezer Holman by name, and lived at

Heathbridge proper; the very Heathbridge I had described, or so my mother believed, for she had never seen her cousin Phillis Green, who was something of an heiress (my father believed), being her father's only child, and old Thomas Green had owned an estate of near upon fifty acres, which must have come to his daughter. My mother's feeling of kinship seemed to have been strongly stirred by the mention of Heathbridge; for my father said she desired me, if ever I went thither again, to make inquiry for the Reverend Ebenezer Holman; and if indeed he lived there, I was further to ask if he had not married one Phillis Green; and if both these questions were answered in the affirmative, I was to go and introduce myself as the only child of Margaret Manning, born Moneypenny. I was enraged at myself for having named Heathbridge at all, when I found what it was drawing down upon me. One Independent minister, as I said to myself, was enough for any man; and here I knew (that is to say, I had been catechized on Sabbath mornings by) Mr Dawson, our minister at home; and I had had to be civil to old Peters at Eltham, and behave myself for five hours running whenever he asked me to tea at his house; and now, just as I felt the free air blowing about me up at Heathbridge, I was to ferret out another minister, and I should perhaps have to be catechized by him, or else asked to tea at his house. Besides, I did not like pushing myself upon strangers, who perhaps had never heard of my mother's name, and such an odd name as it was–Moneypenny; and if they had, had never cared more for her than she had for them, apparently, until this unlucky mention of Heathbridge. Still, I would not disobey my parents in such a trifle, however irksome it might be. So the next time our business took me to Heathbridge, and we were dining in the little sanded inn-parlour, I took the opportunity of Mr Holdsworth's being out of the room, and asked the questions which I was bidden to ask of the rosy-cheeked maid. I was either unintelligible or she was stupid; for she said she did not know, but would ask master; and of course the landlord came in to understand what it was I wanted to know; and I had to bring out all my stammering inquiries before Mr Holdsworth, who would never have attended to them, I dare say, if I had not blushed, and blundered, and made such a fool of myself.

'Yes,' the landlord said, 'the Hope Farm was in Heathbridge proper, and the owner's name was Holman, and he was an Independent minister, and, as far as the landlord could tell, his wife's Christian name was Phillis, anyhow her maiden name was Green.'

'Relations of yours?' asked Mr Holdsworth.

'No, sir–only my mother's second-cousins. Yes, I suppose they are relations. But I never saw them in my life.'

'The Hope Farm is not a stone's throw from here,' said the officious landlord, going to the window. 'If you carry your eye over yon bed of hollyhocks, over the damson-trees in the orchard yonder, you may see a stack of queer-like stone chimneys. Them is the Hope Farm chimneys; it's an old place, though Holman keeps it in good order.'

Mr Holdsworth had risen from the table with more promptitude than I had, and was standing by the window, looking. At the landlord's last words, he turned round, smiling,–'It is not often that parsons know how to keep land in order, is it?'

'Beg pardon, sir, but I must speak as I find; and Minister Holman–we call the Church clergyman here "parson," sir; he would be a bit jealous if he heard a Dissenter called parson–Minister Holman knows what he's about as well as e'er a farmer in the neighbourhood. He gives up five days a week to his own work, and two to the Lord's; and it is difficult to say which he works hardest at. He spends Saturday and Sunday a-writing sermons and a-visiting his flock at Hornby; and at five o'clock on Monday morning he'll be guiding his plough in the Hope Farm yonder just as well as if he could neither read nor write. But your dinner will be getting cold, gentlemen.'

So we went back to table. After a while, Mr Holdsworth broke the silence:–'If I were you, Manning, I'd look up these relations of yours. You can go and see what they're like while we re waiting for Dobson's estimates, and I'll smoke a cigar in the garden meanwhile.'

'Thank you, sir. But I don't know them, and I don't think I want to know them.'

'What did you ask all those questions for, then?' said he, looking quickly up at me. He had no notion of doing or saying things without a purpose. I did not answer, so he continued,–'Make up your mind, and go off and see what this farmer-minister is like, and come back and tell me–I should like to hear.'

I was so in the habit of yielding to his authority, or influence, that I never thought of resisting, but went on my errand, though I remember feeling as if I would rather have had my head cut off. The landlord, who had evidently taken an interest in the event of our discussion in a way that country landlords have, accompanied me to the house-door, and gave me repeated directions, as if I was likely to miss my way in two hundred yards. But I listened to him, for I was glad of the delay, to screw up my courage for the effort of facing unknown people and introducing myself. I went along the lane, I recollect, switching at all the taller roadside weeds, till, after a turn or two, I found myself close in front of the Hope Farm. There was a garden between the house and the shady, grassy lane; I afterwards found that this garden was called the court; perhaps because there was a low wall round it, with an iron railing on the top of the wall, and two great gates between pillars crowned with stone balls for a state entrance to the flagged path leading up to the front door. It was not the habit of the place to go in either by these great gates or by the front door; the gates, indeed, were locked, as I found, though the door stood wide open. I had to go round by a side-path lightly worn on a broad grassy way, which led past the court-wall, past a horse-mount, half covered with stone-crop and the little wild yellow fumitory, to another door–'the curate', as I found it was termed by the master of the house, while the front door, 'handsome and all for show', was termed the 'rector'. I knocked with my hand upon the 'curate' door; a tall girl, about my own age, as I thought, came and opened it, and stood there silent, waiting to know my errand. I see her now–cousin Phillis. The westering sun shone full upon her, and made a slanting stream of light into the room within. She was dressed in dark blue cotton of some kind; up to her throat, down to her wrists, with a little frill of the same wherever it touched her white skin. And such a white skin as it was! I have never seen the like. She had light hair, nearer yellow than any other colour. She looked me steadily in the face with large, quiet eyes, wondering, but untroubled by the sight of a stranger. I thought it odd that so old, so full-grown as she was, she should wear a pinafore over her gown.

Before I had quite made up my mind what to say in reply to her mute inquiry of what I wanted there, a woman's voice called out, 'Who is it, Phillis? If it is any one for butter-milk send them round to the back door.'

I thought I could rather speak to the owner of that voice than to the girl before me; so I passed her, and stood at the entrance of a room hat in hand, for this side-door opened straight into the hall or house-place where the family sate when work was done. There was a brisk little woman of forty or so ironing some huge muslin cravats under the light of a long vine-shaded casement window. She looked at me distrustfully till I began to speak. 'My name is Paul Manning,' said I; but I saw she did not know the name. 'My mother's name was Moneypenny,' said I,–'Margaret Moneypenny.'

'And she married one John Manning, of Birmingham,' said Mrs Holman, eagerly.

'And you'll be her son. Sit down! I am right glad to see you. To think of your being Margaret's son! Why, she was almost a child not so long ago. Well, to be sure, it is five-and-twenty years ago. And what brings you into these parts?'

She sate down herself, as if oppressed by her curiosity as to all the five-and-twenty years that had passed by since she had seen my mother. Her daughter Phillis took up her knitting–a long grey worsted man's stocking, I remember–and knitted away without looking at her work. I felt that the steady gaze of those deep grey eyes was upon me, though once, when I stealthily raised mine to hers, she was examining something on the wall above my head.

When I had answered all my cousin Holman's questions, she heaved a long breath, and said, 'To think of Margaret Moneypenny's boy being in our house! I wish the minister was here. Phillis, in what field is thy father to-day?'

'In the five-acre; they are beginning to cut the corn.'

'He'll not like being sent for, then, else I should have liked you to have seen the minister. But the five-acre is a good step off. You shall have a glass of wine and a bit of cake before you stir from this house, though. You're bound to go, you say, or else the minister comes in mostly when the men have their four o'clock.'

'I must go—I ought to have been off before now.'

'Here, then, Phillis, take the keys.' She gave her daughter some whispered directions, and Phillis left the room.

'She is my cousin, is she not?' I asked. I knew she was, but somehow I wanted to talk of her, and did not know how to begin.

'Yes—Phillis Holman. She is our only child—now.'

Either from that 'now', or from a strange momentary wistfulness in her eyes, I knew that there had been more children, who were now dead.

'How old is cousin Phillis?' said I, scarcely venturing on the new name, it seemed too prettily familiar for me to call her by it; but cousin Holman took no notice of it, answering straight to the purpose.

'Seventeen last May-day; but the minister does not like to hear me calling it May-day,' said she, checking herself with a little awe. 'Phillis was seventeen on the first day of May last,' she repeated in an emended edition.

'And I am nineteen in another month,' thought I, to myself; I don't know why. Then Phillis came in, carrying a tray with wine and cake upon it.

'We keep a house-servant,' said cousin Holman, 'but it is churning day, and she is busy.' It was meant as a little proud apology for her daughter's being the handmaiden.

'I like doing it, mother,' said Phillis, in her grave, full voice.

I felt as if I were somebody in the Old Testament—who, I could not recollect—being served and waited upon by the daughter of the host. Was I like Abraham's servant, when Rebekah gave him to drink at the well? I thought Isaac had not gone the pleasantest way to work in winning him a wife. But Phillis never thought about such things. She was a stately, gracious young woman, in the dress and with the simplicity of a child.

As I had been taught, I drank to the health of my newfound cousin and her husband; and then I ventured to name my cousin Phillis with a little bow of my head towards her; but I was too awkward to look and see how she took my compliment. 'I must go now,' said I, rising.

Neither of the women had thought of sharing in the wine; cousin Holman had broken a bit of cake for form's sake.

'I wish the minister had been within,' said his wife, rising too. Secretly I was very glad he was not. I did not take kindly to ministers in those days, and I thought he must be a particular kind of man, by his objecting to the term May-day. But before I went, cousin Holman made me promise that I would come back on the Saturday following and spend Sunday with them; when I should see something of 'the minister'.

'Come on Friday, if you can,' were her last words as she stood at the curate-door, shading her eyes from the sinking sun with her hand. Inside the house sate cousin Phillis, her golden hair, her dazzling complexion, lighting up the corner of the vine-shadowed room. She had not risen when I bade her good-by; she had looked at me straight as she said her tranquil words of farewell.

I found Mr Holdsworth down at the line, hard at work superintending. As Soon as he had a pause, he said, 'Well, Manning, what are the new cousins like? How do preaching and farming seem to get on together? If the minister turns out to be practical as well as reverend, I shall begin to respect him.'

But he hardly attended to my answer, he was so much more occupied with directing his work-people. Indeed, my answer did not come very readily; and the most distinct part of it was the mention of the invitation that had been given me.

'Oh, of course you can go–and on Friday, too, if you like; there is no reason why not this week; and you've done a long spell of work this time, old fellow.' I thought that I did not want to go on Friday; but when the day came, I found that I should prefer going to staying away, so I availed myself of Mr Holdsworth's permission, and went over to Hope Farm some time in the afternoon, a little later than my last visit. I found the 'curate' open to admit the soft September air, so tempered by the warmth of the sun, that it was warmer out of doors than in, although the wooden log lay smouldering in front of a heap of hot ashes on the hearth. The vine-leaves over the window had a tinge more yellow, their edges were here and there scorched and browned; there was no ironing about, and cousin Holman sate just outside the house, mending a shirt. Phillis was at her knitting indoors: it seemed as if she had been at it all the week. The manyspeckled fowls were pecking about in the farmyard beyond, and the milk-cans glittered with brightness, hung out to sweeten. The court was so full of flowers that they crept out upon the low-covered wall and horse-mount, and were even to be found self-sown upon the turf that bordered the path to the back of the house. I fancied that my Sunday coat was scented for days afterwards by the bushes of sweetbriar and the fraxinella that perfumed the air. From time to time cousin Holman put her hand into a covered basket at her feet, and threw handsful of corn down for the pigeons that cooed and fluttered in the air around, in expectation of this treat.

I had a thorough welcome as soon as she saw me. 'Now this is kind–this is right down friendly,' shaking my hand warmly. 'Phillis, your cousin Manning is come!'

'Call me Paul, will you?' said I; 'they call me so at home, and Manning in the office.'

'Well, Paul, then. Your room is all ready for you, Paul, for, as I said to the minister, "I'll have it ready whether he comes on Friday or not." And the minister said he must go up to the Ashfield whether you were to come or not; but he would come home betimes to see if you were here. I'll show you to your room, and you can wash the dust off a bit.'

After I came down, I think she did not quite know what to do with me; or she might think that I was dull; or she might have work to do in which I hindered her; for she called Phillis, and bade her put on her bonnet, and go with me to the Ashfield, and find father. So we set off, I in a little flutter of a desire to make myself agreeable, but wishing that my companion were not quite so tall; for she was above me in height. While I was wondering how to begin our conversation, she took up the words.

'I suppose, cousin Paul, you have to be very busy at your work all day long in general.'

'Yes, we have to be in the office at half-past eight; and we have an hour for dinner, and then we go at it again till eight or nine.'

'Then you have not much time for reading.'

'No,' said I, with a sudden consciousness that I did not make the most of what leisure I had.

'No more have I. Father always gets an hour before going a-field in the mornings, but mother does not like me to get up so early.'

'My mother is always wanting me to get up earlier when I am at home.'

'What time do you get up?'

'Oh!–ah!–sometimes half-past six: not often though;' for I remembered only twice that I had done so during the past summer.

She turned her head and looked at me.

'Father is up at three; and so was mother till she was ill. I should like to be up at four.'

'Your father up at three! Why, what has he to do at that hour?'

'What has he not to do? He has his private exercise in his own room; he always rings the great bell which calls the men to milking; he rouses up Betty, our maid; as often as not he gives the horses their feed before the man is up–for Jem, who takes care of the horses, is an old man; and father is always loth to disturb him; he looks at the calves, and the shoulders, heels, traces, chaff, and corn before the horses go a-field; he has often to whip-cord the plough-whips; he sees the hogs fed; he looks into the swill-tubs, and writes his orders for what is wanted for food for man and beast; yes, and for fuel, too. And then, if he has a bit of time to spare, he comes in and reads with me–but only English; we keep Latin for the evenings, that we may have time to enjoy it; and then he calls in the men to breakfast, and cuts the boys' bread and cheese; and sees their wooden bottles filled, and sends them off to their work;–and by this time it is half-past six, and we have our breakfast. There is father,' she exclaimed, pointing out to me a man in his shirt-sleeves, taller by the head than the other two with whom he was working. We only saw him through the leaves of the ash-trees growing in the hedge, and I thought I must be confusing the figures, or mistaken: that man still looked like a very powerful labourer, and had none of the precise demureness of appearance which I had always imagined was the characteristic of a minister. It was the Reverend Ebenezer Holman, however. He gave us a nod as we entered the stubble-field; and I think he would have come to meet us but that he was in the middle of giving some directions to his men. I could see that Phillis was built more after his type than her mother's. He, like his daughter, was largely made, and of a fair, ruddy complexion, whereas hers was brilliant and delicate. His hair had been yellow or sandy, but now was grizzled. Yet his grey hairs betokened no failure in strength. I never saw a more powerful man–deep chest, lean flanks, well-planted head. By this time we were nearly up to him; and he interrupted himself and stepped forwards; holding out his hand to me, but addressing Phillis.

'Well, my lass, this is cousin Manning, I suppose. Wait a minute, young man, and I'll put on my coat, and give you a decorous and formal welcome. But–Ned Hall, there ought to be a water-furrow across this land: it's a nasty, stiff, clayey, dauby bit of ground, and thou and I must fall to, come next Monday–I beg your pardon, cousin Manning–and there's old Jem's cottage wants a bit of thatch; you can do that job tomorrow while I am busy.' Then, suddenly changing the tone of his deep bass voice to an odd suggestion of chapels and preachers, he added. 'Now, I will give out the psalm, "Come all harmonious tongues", to be sung to "Mount Ephraim" tune.'

He lifted his spade in his hand, and began to beat time with it; the two labourers seemed to know both words and music, though I did not; and so did Phillis: her rich voice followed her father's as he set the tune; and the men came in with more uncertainty, but still harmoniously. Phillis looked at me once or twice with a little surprise at my silence; but I did not know the words. There we five stood, bareheaded, excepting Phillis, in the tawny stubble-field, from which all the shocks of corn had not yet been carried–a dark wood on one side, where the woodpigeons were cooing; blue distance seen through the ash-trees on the other. Somehow, I think that if I had known the words, and could have sung, my throat would have been choked up by the feeling of the unaccustomed scene.

The hymn was ended, and the men had drawn off before I could stir. I saw the minister beginning to put on his coat, and looking at me with friendly inspection in his gaze, before I could rouse myself.

'I dare say you railway gentlemen don't wind up the day with singing a psalm together,' said he; 'but it is not a bad practice–not a bad practice. We have had it a bit earlier to-day for hospitality's sake–that's all.'

I had nothing particular to say to this, though I was thinking a great deal. From time to time I stole a look at my companion. His coat was black, and so was his waistcoat; neckcloth he had none, his strong full throat being bare above the snow-white shirt. He wore drab-coloured knee-breeches, grey worsted stockings (I thought I knew the maker), and strong-nailed shoes. He carried his hat in his hand, as if he liked to feel the coming breeze lifting his hair. After a while, I saw that the father took hold of the daughter's hand, and so, they holding each other, went along towards home. We had to cross a lane. In it were two little children, one lying prone on the grass in a passion of crying, the other standing stock still, with its finger in its mouth, the large tears slowly rolling down its cheeks for sympathy. The cause of their distress was evident; there was a broken brown pitcher, and a little pool of spilt milk on the road.

'Hollo! Hollo! What's all this?' said the minister. 'why, what have you been about, Tommy,' lifting the little petticoated lad, who was lying sobbing, with one vigorous arm. Tommy looked at him with surprise in his round eyes, but no affright–they were evidently old acquaintances.

'Mammy's jug!' said he, at last, beginning to cry afresh.

'Well! and will crying piece mammy's jug, or pick up spilt milk? How did you manage it, Tommy?'

'He' (jerking his head at the other) 'and me was running races.'

'Tommy said he could beat me,' put in the other.

'Now, I wonder what will make you two silly lads mind, and not run races again with a pitcher of milk between you,' said the minister, as if musing. 'I might flog you, and so save mammy the trouble; for I dare say she'll do it if I don't.' The fresh burst of whimpering from both showed the probability of this.

'Or I might take you to the Hope Farm, and give you some more milk; but then you'd be running races again, and my milk would follow that to the ground, and make another white pool. I think the flogging would be best–don't you?'

'We would never run races no more,' said the elder of the two.

'Then you'd not be boys; you'd be angels.'

'No, we shouldn't.'

'Why not?'

They looked into each other's eyes for an answer to this puzzling question. At length, one said, 'Angels is dead folk.'

'Come; we'll not get too deep into theology. What do you think of my lending you a tin can with a lid to carry the milk home in? That would not break, at any rate; though I would not answer for the milk not spilling if you ran races. That's it!'

He had dropped his daughter's hand, and now held out each of his to the little fellows. Phillis and I followed, and listened to the prattle which the minister's companions now poured out to him, and which he was evidently enjoying. At a certain point, there was a sudden burst of the tawny, ruddy-evening landscape. The minister turned round and quoted a line or two of Latin.

'It's wonderful,' said he, 'how exactly Virgil has hit the enduring epithets, nearly two thousand years ago, and in Italy; and yet how it describes to a T what is now lying before us in the parish of Heathbridge, county——, England.'

'I dare say it does,' said I, all aglow with shame, for I had forgotten the little Latin I ever knew.

The minister shifted his eyes to Phillis's face; it mutely gave him back the sympathetic appreciation that I, in my ignorance, could not bestow.

'Oh! this is worse than the catechism,' thought I; 'that was only remembering words.'

'Phillis, lass, thou must go home with these lads, and tell their mother all about the race and the milk. Mammy must always know the truth,' now speaking to the children. 'And tell her, too, from me that I have got the best birch rod in the parish; and that if she ever thinks her children want a flogging she must bring them to me, and, if I think they deserve it, I'll give it them better than she can.' So Phillis led the children towards the dairy, somewhere in the back yard, and I followed the minister in through the 'curate' into the house-place. 'Their mother,' said he, 'is a bit of a vixen, and apt to punish her children without rhyme or reason. I try to keep the parish rod as well as the parish bull.'

He sate down in the three-cornered chair by the fire-side, and looked around the empty room.

'Where's the missus?' said he to himself. But she was there home–by a look, by a touch, nothing more–as soon as she in a minute;

it was her regular plan to give him his welcome could after his return, and he had missed her now. Regardless of my presence, he went over the day's doings to her; and then, getting up, he said he must go and make himself 'reverend', and that then we would have a cup of tea in the parlour. The parlour was a large room with two casemented windows on the other side of the broad flagged passage leading from the rector-door to the wide staircase, with its shallow, polished oaken steps, on which no carpet was ever laid. The parlour-floor was covered in the middle by a home-made carpeting of needlework and list. One or two quaint family pictures of the Holman family hung round the walls; the fire-grate and irons were much ornamented with brass; and on a table against the wall between the windows, a great beau-pot of flowers was placed upon the folio volumes of Matthew Henry's Bible. It was a compliment to me to use this room, and I tried to be grateful for it; but we never had our meals there after that first day, and I was glad of it; for the large house-place, living room, dining-room, whichever you might like to call it, was twice as comfortable and cheerful. There was a rug in front of the great large fire-place, and an oven by the grate, and a crook, with the kettle hanging from it, over the bright wood-fire; everything that ought to be black and Polished in that room was black and Polished; and the flags, and window-curtains, and such things as were to be white and clean, were just spotless in their purity. Opposite to the fire-place, extending the whole length of the room, was an oaken shovel-board, with the right incline for a skilful player to send the weights into the prescribed space. There were baskets of white work about, and a small shelf of books hung against the wall, books used for reading, and not for propping up a beau-pot of flowers. I took down one or two of those books once when I was left alone in the house-place on the first evening–Virgil, Caesar, a Greek grammar–oh, dear! ah, me! and Phillis Holman's name in each of them! I shut them up, and put them back in their places, and walked as far away from the bookshelf as I could. Yes, and I gave my cousin Phillis a wide berth, as though she was sitting at her work quietly enough, and her hair was looking more golden, her dark eyelashes longer, her round pillar of a throat whiter than ever. We had done tea, and we had returned into the house-place that the minister might smoke his pipe without fear of contaminating the drab damask window-curtains of the parlour. He had made himself 'reverend' by putting on one of the voluminous white muslin neckcloths that I had seen cousin Holman ironing that first visit I had paid to the Hope Farm, and by making one or two other unimportant changes in his dress. He sate looking steadily at me, but whether he saw me or not I cannot tell. At the time I fancied that he did, and was gauging me in some unknown fashion in his secret mind. Every now and then he took his pipe out of his mouth, knocked out the ashes, and asked me some fresh question. As long as these related to my acquirements or my reading, I shuffled uneasily and did not know what to answer. By-and-by he got round to the more practical subject of railroads, and on this I was more at home. I really had taken an interest in my work; nor would Mr Holdsworth, indeed, have kept me in his employment if I had not given my mind as well as my time to it; and I was, besides, full of the difficulties which beset us just then, owing to our not being able to find a steady bottom on the Heathbridge moss, over which we wished to carry our line. In the midst of all my eagerness in speaking about this, I could not help being struck with the extreme pertinence of his questions. I do not mean that he did not show ignorance of many of the details of engineering: that was to have been expected; but on the premises he had got hold of; he thought clearly and reasoned logically. Phillis—so like him as she was both in body and mind—kept stopping at her work and looking at me, trying to fully understand all that I said. I felt she did; and perhaps it made me take more pains in using clear expressions, and arranging my words, than I otherwise should.

'She shall see I know something worth knowing, though it mayn't be her dead-and-gone languages,' thought I.

'I see,' said the minister, at length. 'I understand it all. You've a clear, good head of your own, my lad,—choose how you came by it.'

'From my father,' said I, proudly. 'Have you not heard of his discovery of a new method of shunting? It was in the Gazette. It was patented. I thought every one had heard of Manning's patent winch.'

'We don't know who invented the alphabet,' said he, half smiling, and taking up his pipe.

'No, I dare say not, sir,' replied I, half offended; 'that's so long ago.' Puff–puff–puff.

'But your father must be a notable man. I heard of him once before; and it is not many a one fifty miles away whose fame reaches Heathbridge.'

'My father is a notable man, sir. It is not me that says so; it is Mr Holdsworth, and–and everybody.'

'He is right to stand up for his father,' said cousin Holman, as if she were pleading for me.

I chafed inwardly, thinking that my father needed no one to stand up for him. He was man sufficient for himself.

'Yes–he is right,' said the minister, placidly. 'Right, because it comes from his heart–right, too, as I believe, in point of fact. Else there is many a young cockerel that will stand upon a dunghill and crow about his father, by way of making his own plumage to shine. I should like to know thy father,' he went on, turning straight to me, with a kindly, frank look in his eyes.

But I was vexed, and would take no notice. Presently, having finished his pipe, he got up and left the room. Phillis put her work hastily down, and went after him. In a minute or two she returned, and sate down again. Not long after, and before I had quite recovered my good temper, he opened the door out of which he had passed, and called to me to come to him. I went across a narrow stone passage into a strange, many-cornered room, not ten feet in area, part study, part counting house, looking into the farm-yard; with a desk to sit at, a desk to stand at, a Spittoon, a set of shelves with old divinity books upon them; another, smaller, filled with books on farriery, farming, manures, and such subjects, with pieces of paper containing memoranda stuck against the whitewashed walls with wafers, nails, pins, anything that came readiest to hand; a box of carpenter's tools on the floor, and some manuscripts in short-hand on the desk.

He turned round, half laughing. 'That foolish girl of mine thinks I have vexed you'–putting his large, powerful hand on my shoulder. '"Nay," says I, "kindly meant is kidney taken"–is it not so?'

'It was not quite, sir,' replied I, vanquished by his manner; 'but it shall be in future.'

'Come, that's right. You and I shall be friends. Indeed, it's not many a one I would bring in here. But I was reading a book this morning, and I could not make it out; it is a book that was left here by mistake one day; I had subscribed to Brother Robinson's sermons; and I was glad to see this instead of them, for sermons though they be, they're . . . well, never mind! I took 'em both, and made my old coat do a bit longer; but all's fish that comes to my net. I have fewer books than leisure to read them, and I have a prodigious big appetite. Here it is.'

It was a volume of stiff mechanics, involving many technical terms, and some rather deep mathematics. These last, which would have puzzled me, seemed easy enough to him; all that he wanted was the explanations of the technical words, which I could easily give.

While he was looking through the book to find the places where he had been puzzled, my wandering eye caught on some of the papers on the wall, and I could not help reading one, which has stuck by me ever since. At first, it seemed a kind of weekly diary; but then I saw that the seven days were portioned out for special prayers and intercessions: Monday for his family, Tuesday for enemies, Wednesday for the Independent churches, Thursday for all other churches, Friday for persons afflicted, Saturday for his own soul, Sunday for all wanderers and sinners, that they might be brought home to the fold.

We were called back into the house-place to have supper. A door opening into the kitchen was opened; and all stood up in both rooms, while the minister, tall, large, one hand resting on the spread table, the other lifted up, said, in the deep voice that would have been loud had it not been so full and rich, but without the peculiar accent or twang that I believe is considered devout by some people, 'Whether we eat or drink, or whatsoever we do, let us do all to the glory of God.'

The supper was an immense meat-pie. We of the house-place were helped first; then the minister hit the handle of his buck-horn carving-knife on the table once, and said,–

'Now or never,' which meant, did any of us want any more; and when we had all declined, either by silence or by words, he knocked twice with his knife on the table, and Betty came in through the open door, and carried off the great dish to the kitchen, where an old man and a young one, and a help-girl, were awaiting their meal.

'Shut the door, if you will,' said the minister to Betty.

'That's in honour of you,' said cousin Holman, in a tone of satisfaction, as the door was shut. 'when we've no stranger with us, the minister is so fond of keeping the door Open, and talking to the men and maids, just as much as to Phillis and me.

'It brings us all together like a household just before we meet as a household in prayer,' said he, in explanation. 'But to go back to what we were talking about–can you tell me of any simple book on dynamics that I could put in my pocket, and study a little at leisure times in the day?'

'Leisure times, father?' said Phillis, with a nearer approach to a smile than I had yet seen on her face.

'Yes; leisure times, daughter. There is many an odd minute lost in waiting for other folk; and now that railroads are coming so near us, it behoves us to know something about them.'

I thought of his own description of his 'prodigious big appetite' for learning. And he had a good appetite of his own for the more material victual before him. But I saw, or fancied I saw, that he had some rule for himself in the matter both of food and drink.

As soon as supper was done the household assembled for prayer. It was a long impromptu evening prayer; and it would have seemed desultory enough had I not had a glimpse of the kind of day that preceded it, and so been able to find a clue to the thoughts that preceded the disjointed utterances; for he kept there kneeling down in the centre of a circle, his eyes shut, his outstretched hands pressed palm to palm–sometimes with a long pause of silence was anything else he wished to 'lay before the Lord! (to use his own expression)–before he concluded with the blessing. He prayed for the cattle and live creatures, rather to my surprise; for my attention had begun to wander, till it was recalled by the familiar words.

And here I must not forget to name an odd incident at the conclusion of the prayer, and before we had risen from our knees (indeed before Betty was well awake, for she made a practice of having a sound nap, her weary head lying on her stalwart arms); the minister, still kneeling in our midst, but with his eyes wide open, and his arms dropped by his side, spoke to the elder man, who turned round on his knees to attend.

'John, didst see that Daisy had her warm mash to-night; for we must not neglect the means, John—two quarts of gruel, a spoonful of ginger, and a gill of beer—the poor beast needs it, and I fear it slipped Out of my mind to tell thee; and here was I asking a blessing and neglecting the means, which is a mockery,' said he, dropping his voice. Before we went to bed he told me he should see little or nothing more of me during my visit, which was to end on Sunday evening, as he always gave up both Saturday and Sabbath to his work in the ministry. I remembered that the landlord at the inn had told me this on the day when I first inquired about these new relations of mine; and I did not dislike the opportunity which I saw would be afforded me of becoming more acquainted with cousin Holman and Phillis, though I earnestly hoped that the latter would not attack me on the subject of the dead languages.

I went to bed, and dreamed that I was as tall as cousin Phillis, and had a sudden and miraculous growth of whisker, and a still more miraculous acquaintance with Latin and Greek. Alas! I wakened up still a short, beardless lad, with 'tempus fugit' for my sole remembrance of the little Latin I had once learnt. While I was dressing, a bright thought came over me: I could question cousin Phillis, instead of her questioning me, and so manage to keep the choice of the subjects of conversation in my own power.

Early as it was, every one had breakfasted, and my basin of bread and milk was put on the oven-top to await my coming down. Every one was gone about their work. The first to come into the house-place was Phillis with a basket of eggs. Faithful to my resolution, I asked,—

'What are those?'

She looked at me for a moment, and then said gravely,—

'Potatoes!'

'No! they are not,' said I. 'They are eggs. What do you mean by saying they are potatoes?'

'What do you mean by asking me what they were, when they were plain to be seen?' retorted she.

We were both getting a little angry with each other.

'I don't know. I wanted to begin to talk to you; and I was afraid you would talk to me about books as you did yesterday. I have not read much; and you and the minister have read so much.'

'I have not,' said she. 'But you are our guest; and mother says I must make it pleasant to you. We won't talk of books. What must we talk about?'

'I don't know. How old are you?'

'Seventeen last May. How old are you?'

'I am nineteen. Older than you by nearly two years,' said I, drawing myself up to my full height.

'I should not have thought you were above sixteen,' she replied, as quietly as if she were not saying the most provoking thing she possibly could. Then came a pause.

'What are you going to do now?' asked I.

'I should be dusting the bed-chambers; but mother said I had better stay and make it pleasant to you,' said she, a little plaintively, as if dusting rooms was far the easiest task.

'Will you take me to see the live-stock? I like animals, though I don't know much about them.'

'Oh, do you? I am so glad! I was afraid you would not like animals, as you did not like books.'

I wondered why she said this. I think it was because she had begun to fancy all our tastes must be dissimilar. We went together all through the farm-yard; we fed the poultry, she kneeling down with her pinafore full of corn and meal, and tempting the little timid, downy chickens upon it, much to the anxiety of the fussy ruffled hen, their mother. She called to the pigeons, who fluttered down at the sound of her voice. She and I examined the great sleek cart-horses; sympathized in our dislike of pigs; fed the calves; coaxed the sick cow, Daisy; and admired the others out at pasture; and came back tired and hungry and dirty at dinner-time, having quite forgotten that there were such things as dead languages, and consequently capital friends.

Part II

Cousin Holman gave me the weekly county newspaper to read aloud to her, while she mended stockings out of a high piled-up basket, Phillis helping her mother. I read and read, unregardful of the words I was uttering, thinking of all manner of other things; of the bright colour of Phillis's hair, as the afternoon sun fell on her bending head; of the silence of the house, which enabled me to hear the double tick of the old clock which stood half-way up the stairs; of the variety of inarticulate noises which cousin Holman made while I read, to show her sympathy, wonder, or horror at the newspaper intelligence. The tranquil monotony of that hour made me feel as if I had lived for ever, and should live for ever droning out paragraphs in that warm sunny room, with my two quiet hearers, and the curled-up pussy cat sleeping on the hearth-rug, and the clock on the house-stairs perpetually clicking out the passage of the moments. By-and-by Betty the servant came to the door into the kitchen, and made a sign to Phillis, who put her half-mended stocking down, and went away to the kitchen without a word. Looking at cousin Holman a minute or two afterwards, I saw that she had dropped her chin upon her breast, and had fallen fast asleep. I put the newspaper down, and was nearly following her example, when a waft of air from some unseen source, slightly opened the door of communication with the kitchen, that Phillis must have left unfastened; and I saw part of her figure as she sate by the dresser, peeling apples with quick dexterity of finger, but with repeated turnings of her head towards some book lying on the dresser by her. I softly rose, and as softly went into the kitchen, and looked over her shoulder; before she was aware of my neighbourhood, I had seen that the book was in a language unknown to me, and the running title was L'Inferno. Just as I was making out the relationship of this word to 'infernal', she started and turned round, and, as if continuing her thought as she spoke, she sighed out,–

'Oh! it is so difficult! Can you help me?' putting her finger below a line.

'Me! I! I don't even know what language it is in!'

'Don't you see it is Dante?' she replied, almost petulantly; she did so want help.

'Italian, then?' said I, dubiously; for I was not quite sure.

'Yes. And I do so want to make it out. Father can help me a little, for he knows Latin; but then he has so little time.'

'You have not much, I should think, if you have often to try and do two things at once, as you are doing now.

'Oh! that's nothing! Father bought a heap of old books cheap. And I knew something about Dante before; and I have always liked Virgil so much. Paring apples is nothing, if I could only make out this old Italian. I wish you knew it.'

'I wish I did,' said I, moved by her impetuosity of tone. 'If, now, only Mr Holdsworth were here; he can speak Italian like anything, I believe.'

'Who is Mr Holdsworth?' said Phillis, looking up.

'Oh, he's our head engineer. He's a regular first-rate fellow! He can do anything;' my hero-worship and my pride in my chief all coming into play. Besides, if I was not clever and book-learned myself, it was something to belong to some one who was.

'How is it that he speaks Italian?' asked Phillis.

'He had to make a railway through Piedmont, which is in Italy, I believe; and he had to talk to all the workmen in Italian; and I have heard him say that for nearly two years he had only Italian books to read in the queer outlandish places he was in.'

'Oh, dear!' said Phillis; 'I wish–' and then she stopped. I was not quite sure whether to say the next thing that came into my mind; but I said it.

'Could I ask him anything about your book, or your difficulties?'

She was silent for a minute or so, and then she made reply,–

'No! I think not. Thank you very much, though. I can generally puzzle a thing out in time. And then, perhaps, I remember it better than if some one had helped me. I'll put it away now, and you must move off, for I've got to make the paste for the pies; we always have a cold dinner on Sabbaths.'

'But I may stay and help you, mayn't I?'

'Oh, yes; not that you can help at all, but I like to have you with me.'
I was both flattered and annoyed at this straightforward avowal. I was
pleased that she liked me; but I was young coxcomb enough to have
wished to play the lover, and I was quite wise enough to perceive that
if she had any idea of the kind in her head she would never have
spoken out so frankly. I comforted myself immediately, however, by
finding out that the grapes were sour. A great tall girl in a pinafore, half
a head taller than I was, reading books that I had never heard of, and
talking about them too, as of far more interest than any mere personal
subjects; that was the last day on which I ever thought of my dear
cousin Phillis as the possible mistress of my heart and life. But we were
all the greater friends for this idea being utterly put away and buried out
of sight.

Late in the evening the minister came home from Hornby. He had
been calling on the different members of his flock; and unsatisfactory
work it had proved to him, it seemed from the fragments that dropped
out of his thoughts into his talk.

'I don't see the men; they are all at their business, their shops, or
their warehouses; they ought to be there. I have no fault to find with
them; only if a pastor's teaching or words of admonition are good for
anything, they are needed by the men as much as by the women.'

'Cannot you go and see them in their places of business, and remind
them of their Christian privileges and duties, minister?' asked cousin
Holman, who evidently thought that her husband's words could never
be out of place.

'No!' said he, shaking his head. 'I judge them by myself. If there are
clouds in the sky, and I am getting in the hay just ready for loading, and
rain sure to come in the night, I should look ill upon brother Robinson
if he came into the field to speak about serious things.'

'But, at any rate, father, you do good to the women, and perhaps they
repeat what you have said to them to their husbands and children?'

'It is to be hoped they do, for I cannot reach the men directly; but the
women are apt to tarry before coming to me, to put on ribbons and
gauds; as if they could hear the message I bear to them best in their
smart clothes. Mrs Dobson to-day–Phillis, I am thankful thou dost not

care for the vanities of dress!' Phillis reddened a little as she said, in a low humble voice,–

'But I do, father, I'm afraid. I often wish I could wear pretty-coloured ribbons round my throat like the squire's daughters.'

'It's but natural, minister!' said his wife; 'I'm not above liking a silk gown better than a cotton one myself!'

'The love of dress is a temptation and a snare,' said he, gravely. 'The true adornment is a meek and quiet spirit. And, wife,' said he, as a sudden thought crossed his mind, 'in that matter I, too, have sinned. I wanted to ask you, could we not sleep in the grey room, instead of our own?'

'Sleep in the grey room?–change our room at this time o' day?' cousin Holman asked, in dismay.

'Yes,' said he. 'It would save me from a daily temptation to anger. Look at my chin!' he continued; 'I cut it this morning–I cut it on Wednesday when I was shaving; I do not know how many times I have cut it of late, and all from impatience at seeing Timothy Cooper at his work in the yard.'

'He's a downright lazy tyke!' said cousin Holman. 'He's not worth his wage. There's but little he can do, and what he can do, he does badly.'

'True,' said the minister. 'He is but, so to speak, a half-wit; and yet he has got a wife and children.'

'More shame for him!'

'But that is past change. And if I turn him off; no one else will take him on. Yet I cannot help watching him of a morning as he goes sauntering about his work in the yard; and I watch, and I watch, till the old Adam rises strong within me at his lazy ways, and some day, I am afraid, I shall go down and send him about his business–let alone the way in which he makes me cut myself while I am shaving–and then his wife and children will starve. I wish we could move to the grey room.'

I do not remember much more of my first visit to the Hope Farm. We went to chapel in Heathbridge, slowly and decorously walking along the lanes, ruddy and tawny with the colouring of the coming autumn. The minister walked a little before us, his hands behind his back, his head bent down, thinking about the discourse to be delivered to his people, cousin Holman said; and we spoke low and quietly, in order not to interrupt his thoughts. But I could not help noticing the respectful greetings which he received from both rich and poor as we went along; greetings which he acknowledged with a kindly wave of his hand, but with no words of reply. As we drew near the town, I could see some of the young fellows we met cast admiring looks on Phillis; and that made me look too. She had on a white gown, and a short black silk cloak, according to the fashion of the day. A straw bonnet with brown ribbon strings; that was all. But what her dress wanted in colour, her sweet bonny face had. The walk made her cheeks bloom like the rose; the very whites of her eyes had a blue tinge in them, and her dark eyelashes brought out the depth of the blue eyes themselves. Her yellow hair was put away as straight as its natural curliness would allow. If she did not perceive the admiration she excited, I am sure cousin Holman did; for she looked as fierce and as proud as ever her quiet face could look, guarding her treasure, and yet glad to perceive that others could see that it was a treasure. That afternoon I had to return to Eltham to be ready for the next day's work. I found out afterwards that the minister and his family were all 'exercised in spirit,' as to whether they did well in asking me to repeat my visits at the Hope Farm, seeing that of necessity I must return to Eltham on the Sabbath-day. However, they did go on asking me, and I went on visiting them, whenever my other engagements permitted me, Mr Holdsworth being in this case, as in all, a kind and indulgent friend. Nor did my new acquaintances oust him from my strong regard and admiration. I had room in my heart for all, I am happy to say, and as far as I can remember, I kept praising each to the other in a manner which, if I had been an older man, living more amongst people of the world, I should have thought unwise, as well as a little ridiculous. It was unwise, certainly, as it was almost sure to cause disappointment if ever they did become acquainted; and perhaps it was ridiculous, though I do not think we any of us thought it so at the time. The minister used to listen to my accounts of Mr Holdsworth's many accomplishments and various adventures in travel with the truest interest, and most kindly good faith; and Mr Holdsworth in return liked to hear about my visits to the farm, and description of my cousin's life there–liked it, I mean, as much as he liked anything that was merely narrative, without leading to action.

So I went to the farm certainly, on an average, once a month during that autumn; the course of life there was so peaceful and quiet, that I can only remember one small event, and that was one that I think I took more notice of than any one else: Phillis left off wearing the pinafores that had always been so obnoxious to me; I do not know why they were banished, but on one of my visits I found them replaced by pretty linen aprons in the morning, and a black silk one in the afternoon. And the blue cotton gown became a brown stuff one as winter drew on; this sounds like some book I once read, in which a migration from the blue bed to the brown was spoken of as a great family event.

Towards Christmas my dear father came to see me, and to consult Mr Holdsworth about the improvement which has since been known as 'Manning's driving wheel'. Mr Holdsworth, as I think I have before said, had a very great regard for my father, who had been employed in the same great machine-shop in which Mr Holdsworth had served his apprenticeship; and he and my father had many mutual jokes about one of these gentlemen-apprentices who used to set about his smith's work in white wash-leather gloves, for fear of spoiling his hands. Mr Holdsworth often spoke to me about my father as having the same kind of genius for mechanical invention as that of George Stephenson, and my father had come over now to consult him about several improvements, as well as an offer of partnership. It was a great pleasure to me to see the mutual regard of these two men. Mr Holdsworth, young, handsome, keen, well-dressed, an object of admiration to all the youth of Eltham; my father, in his decent but unfashionable Sunday clothes, his plain, sensible face full of hard lines, the marks of toil and thought,–his hands, blackened beyond the power of soap and water by years of labour in the foundry; speaking a strong Northern dialect, while Mr Holdsworth had a long soft drawl in his voice, as many of the Southerners have, and was reckoned in Eltham to give himself airs.

Although most of my father's leisure time was occupied with conversations about the business I have mentioned, he felt that he ought not to leave Eltham without going to pay his respects to the s who had been so kind to his son. So he and I ran up on an engine along the incomplete line as far as Heathbridge, and went, by invitation, to spend a day at the farm.

It was odd and yet pleasant to me to perceive how these two men, each having led up to this point such totally dissimilar lives, seemed to come together by instinct, after one quiet straight look into each other's faces. My father was a thin, wiry man of five foot seven; the minister was a broad-shouldered, fresh-coloured man of six foot one; they were neither of them great talkers in general—perhaps the minister the most so—but they spoke much to each other. My father went into the fields with the minister; I think I see him now, with his hands behind his back, listening intently to all explanations of tillage, and the different processes of farming; occasionally taking up an implement, as if unconsciously, and examining it with a critical eye, and now and then asking a question, which I could see was considered as pertinent by his companion. Then we returned to look at the cattle, housed and bedded in expectation of the snow-storm hanging black on the western horizon, and my father learned the points of a cow with as much attention as if he meant to turn farmer. He had his little book that he used for mechanical memoranda and measurements in his pocket, and he took it out to write down 'straight back', small muzzle', 'deep barrel', and I know not what else, under the head 'cow'. He was very critical on a turnip-cutting machine, the clumsiness of which first incited him to talk; and when we went into the house he sate thinking and quiet for a bit, while Phillis and her mother made the last preparations for tea, with a little unheeded apology from cousin Holman, because we were not sitting in the best parlour, which she thought might be chilly on so cold a night. I wanted nothing better than the blazing, crackling fire that sent a glow over all the house-place, and warmed the snowy flags under our feet till they seemed to have more heat than the crimson rug right in front of the fire. After tea, as Phillis and I were talking together very happily, I heard an irrepressible exclamation from cousin Holman,—

'Whatever is the man about!'

And on looking round, I saw my father taking a straight burning stick out of the fire, and, after waiting for a minute, and examining the charred end to see if it was fitted for his purpose, he went to the hard-wood dresser, scoured to the last pitch of whiteness and cleanliness, and began drawing with the stick; the best substitute for chalk or charcoal within his reach, for his pocket-book pencil was not strong or bold enough for his purpose. When he had done, he began to explain his new model of a turnip-cutting machine to the minister, who had been watching him in silence all the time. Cousin Holman had, in the meantime, taken a duster out of a drawer, and, under pretence of being as much interested as her husband in the drawing, was secretly trying on an outside mark how easily it would come off, and whether it would leave her dresser as white as before. Then Phillis was sent for the book on dynamics about which I had been consulted during my first visit, and my father had to explain many difficulties, which he did in language as clear as his mind, making drawings with his stick wherever they were needed as illustrations, the minister sitting with his massive head resting on his hands, his elbows on the table, almost unconscious of Phillis, leaning over and listening greedily, with her hand on his shoulder, sucking in information like her father's own daughter. I was rather sorry for cousin Holman; I had been so once or twice before; for do what she would, she was completely unable even to understand the pleasure her husband and daughter took in intellectual pursuits, much less to care in the least herself for the pursuits themselves, and was thus unavoidably thrown out of some of their interests. I had once or twice thought she was a little jealous of her own child, as a fitter companion for her husband than she was herself; and I fancied the minister himself was aware of this feeling, for I had noticed an occasional sudden change of subject, and a tenderness of appeal in his voice as he spoke to her, which always made her look contented and peaceful again. I do not think that Phillis ever perceived these little shadows; in the first place, she had such complete reverence for her parents that she listened to them both as if they had been St Peter and St Paul; and besides, she was always too much engrossed with any matter in hand to think about other people's manners and looks.

This night I could see, though she did not, how much she was winning on my father. She asked a few questions which showed that she had followed his explanations up to that point; possibly, too, her unusual beauty might have something to do with his favourable impression of her; but he made no scruple of expressing his admiration of her to her father and mother in her absence from the room; and from that evening I date a project of his which came out to me a day or two afterwards, as we sate in my little three-cornered room in Eltham. 'Paul,' he began, 'I never thought to be a rich man; but I think it's coming upon me. Some folk are making a deal of my new machine (calling it by its technical name), and Ellison, of the Borough Green Works, has gone so far as to ask me to be his partner.'

'Mr Ellison the Justice!–who lives in King Street? why, he drives his carriage!' said I, doubting, yet exultant.

'Ay, lad, John Ellison. But that's no sign that I shall drive my carriage. Though I should like to save thy mother walking, for she's not so young as she was. But that's a long way off; anyhow. I reckon I should start with a third profit. It might be seven hundred, or it might be more. I should like to have the power to work out some fancies o' mine. I care for that much more than for th' brass. And Ellison has no lads; and by nature the business would come to thee in course o' time. Ellison's lasses are but bits o' things, and are not like to come by husbands just yet; and when they do, maybe they'll not be in the mechanical line. It will be an opening for thee, lad, if thou art steady. Thou'rt not great shakes, I know, in th' inventing line; but many a one gets on better without having fancies for something he does not see and never has seen. I'm right down glad to see that mother's cousins are such uncommon folk for sense and goodness. I have taken the minister to my heart like a brother; and she is a womanly quiet sort of a body. And I'll tell you frank, Paul, it will be a happy day for me if ever you can come and tell me that Phillis Holman is like to be my daughter. I think if that lass had not a penny, she would be the making of a man; and she'll have yon house and lands, and you may be her match yet in fortune if all goes well.'

I was growing as red as fire; I did not know what to say, and yet I wanted to say something; but the idea of having a wife of my own at some future day, though it had often floated about in my own head, sounded so strange when it was thus first spoken about by my father. He saw my confusion, and half smiling said,–

'Well, lad, what dost say to the old father's plans? Thou art but young, to be sure; but when I was thy age, I would ha' given my right hand if I might ha' thought of the chance of wedding the lass I cared for–'

'My mother?' asked I, a little struck by the change of his tone of voice.

'No! not thy mother. Thy mother is a very good woman–none better. No! the lass I cared for at nineteen ne'er knew how I loved her, and a year or two after and she was dead, and ne'er knew. I think she would ha' been glad to ha' known it, poor Molly; but I had to leave the place where we lived for to try to earn my bread and I meant to come back but before ever I did, she was dead and gone: I ha' never gone there since. But if you fancy Phillis Holman, and can get her to fancy you, my lad, it shall go different with you, Paul, to what it did with your father.'

I took counsel with myself very rapidly, and I came to a clear conclusion. 'Father,' said I, 'if I fancied Phillis ever so much, she would never fancy me. I like her as much as I could like a sister; and she likes me as if I were her brother–her younger brother.'

I could see my father's countenance fall a little.

'You see she's so clever she's more like a man than a woman–she knows Latin and Greek.'

'She'd forget 'em, if she'd a houseful of children,' was my father's comment on this.

'But she knows many a thing besides, and is wise as well as learned; she has been so much with her father. She would never think much of me, and I should like my wife to think a deal of her husband.'

'It is not just book-learning or the want of it as makes a wife think much or little of her husband,' replied my father, evidently unwilling to give up a project which had taken deep root in his mind. 'It's a something I don't rightly know how to call it–if he's manly, and sensible, and straightforward; and I reckon you're that, my boy.'

'I don't think I should like to have a wife taller than I am, father,' said I, smiling; he smiled too, but not heartily.

'Well,' said he, after a pause. 'It's but a few days I've been thinking of it, but I'd got as fond of my notion as if it had been a new engine as

I'd been planning out. Here's our Paul, thinks I to myself, a good sensible breed o' lad, as has never vexed or troubled his mother or me; with a good business opening out before him, age nineteen, not so bad-looking, though perhaps not to call handsome, and here's his cousin, not too near cousin, but just nice, as one may say; aged seventeen, good and true, and well brought up to work with her hands as well as her head; a scholar–but that can't be helped, and is more her misfortune than her fault, seeing she is the only child of scholar–and as I said afore, once she's a wife and a she'll forget it all, I'll be bound–with a good fortune in land and house when it shall please the Lord to take her parents to himself; with eyes like poor Molly's for beauty, a colour that comes and goes on a milk-white skin, and as pretty a mouth–,

'Why, Mr Manning, what fair lady are you describing?' asked Mr Holdsworth, who had come quickly and suddenly upon our tete-a-tete, and had caught my father's last words as he entered the room. Both my father and I felt rather abashed; it was such an odd subject for us to be talking about; but my father, like a straightforward simple man as he was, spoke out the truth.

'I've been telling Paul of Ellison's offer, and saying how good an opening it made for him–'

'I wish I'd as good,' said Mr Holdsworth. 'But has the business a "pretty mouth"?'

'You're always so full of your joking, Mr Holdsworth,' said my father. 'I was going to say that if he and his cousin Phillis Holman liked to make it up between them, I would put no spoke in the wheel.'

'Phillis Holman!' said Mr Holdsworth. 'Is she the daughter of the minister-farmer out at Heathbridge? Have I been helping on the course of true love by letting you go there so often? I knew nothing of it.'

'There is nothing to know,' said I, more annoyed than I chose to show. 'There is no more true love in the case than may be between the first brother and sister you may choose to meet. I have been telling father she would never think of me; she's a great deal taller and cleverer; and I'd rather be taller and more learned than my wife when I have one.'

'And it is she, then, that has the pretty mouth your father spoke about? I should think that would be an antidote to the cleverness and learning. But I ought to apologize for breaking in upon your last night; I came upon business to your father.'

And then he and my father began to talk about many things that had no interest for me just then, and I began to go over again my conversation with my father. The more I thought about it, the more I felt that I had spoken truly about my feelings towards Phillis Holman. I loved her dearly as a sister, but I could never fancy her as my wife. Still less could I think of her ever–yes, condescending, that is the word–condescending to marry me. I was roused from a reverie on what I should like my possible wife to be, by hearing my father's warm praise of the minister, as a most unusual character; how they had got back from the diameter of driving-wheels to the subject of the Holmans I could never tell; but I saw that my father's weighty praises were exciting some curiosity in Mr Holdsworth's mind; indeed, he said, almost in a voice of reproach,–

'Why, Paul, you never told me what kind of a fellow this minister-cousin of yours was!'

'I don't know that I found out, sir,' said I. 'But if I had, I don't think you'd have listened to me, as you have done to my father.'

'No! most likely not, old fellow,' replied Mr Holdsworth, laughing. And again and afresh I saw what a handsome pleasant clear face his was; and though this evening I had been a bit put out with him–through his sudden coming, and his having heard my father's open-hearted confidence–my hero resumed all his empire over me by his bright merry laugh.

And if he had not resumed his old place that night, he would have done so the next day, when, after my father's departure, Mr Holdsworth spoke about him with such just respect for his character, such ungrudging admiration of his great mechanical genius, that I was compelled to say, almost unawares,–

'Thank you, sir. I am very much obliged to you.'

'Oh, you're not at all. I am only speaking the truth. Here's a Birmingham workman, self-educated, one may say–having never associated with stimulating minds, or had what advantages travel and contact with the world may be supposed to afford–working out his own thoughts into steel and iron, making a scientific name for himself–a fortune, if it pleases him to work for money–and keeping his singleness of heart, his perfect simplicity of manner; it puts me out of patience to think of my expensive schooling, my travels hither and thither, my heaps of scientific books, and I have done nothing to speak of. But it's evidently good blood; there's that Mr Holman, that cousin of yours, made of the same stuff'

'But he's only cousin because he married my mother's second cousin,' said I.

'That knocks a pretty theory on the head, and twice over, too. I should like to make Holman's acquaintance.'

'I am sure they would be so glad to see you at Hope Farm,' said I, eagerly. 'In fact, they've asked me to bring you several times: only I thought you would find it dull.'

'Not at all. I can't go yet though, even if you do get me an invitation; for the — Company want me to go to the — Valley, and look over the ground a bit for them, to see if it would do for a branch line; it's a job which may take me away for some time; but I shall be backwards and forwards, and you're quite up to doing what is needed in my absence; the only work that may be beyond you is keeping old Jevons from drinking.' He went on giving me directions about the management of the men employed on the line, and no more was said then, or for several months, about his going to Rope Farm. He went off into — Valley, a dark overshadowed dale, where the sun seemed to set behind the hills before four o'clock on midsummer afternoon. Perhaps it was this that brought on the attack of low fever which he had soon after the beginning of the new year; he was very ill for many weeks, almost many months; a married sister–his only relation, I think–came down from London to nurse him, and I went over to him when I could, to see him, and give him 'masculine news,' as he called it; reports of the progress of the line, which, I am glad to say, I was able to carry on in his absence, in the slow gradual way which suited the company best, while trade was in a languid state, and money dear in the market. Of course, with this occupation for my scanty leisure, I did not often go over to Hope Farm. Whenever I did go, I met with a thorough welcome; and many inquiries were made as to Holdsworth's illness, and the progress of his recovery.

At length, in June I think it was, he was sufficiently recovered to come back to his lodgings at Eltham, and resume part at least of his work. His sister, Mrs Robinson, had been obliged to leave him some weeks before, owing to some epidemic amongst her own children. As long as I had seen Mr Holdsworth in the rooms at the little inn at Hensleydale, where I had been accustomed to look upon him as an invalid, I had not been aware of the visible shake his fever had given to his health. But, once back in the old lodgings, where I had always seen him so buoyant, eloquent, decided, and vigorous in former days, my spirits sank at the change in one whom I had always regarded with a strong feeling of admiring affection. He sank into silence and despondency after the least exertion; he seemed as if he could not make up his mind to any action, or else that, when it was made up, he lacked strength to carry out his purpose. Of course, it was but the natural state of slow convalescence, after so sharp an illness; but, at the time, I did not know this, and perhaps I represented his state as more serious than it was to my kind relations at Hope Farm; who, in their grave, simple, eager way, immediately thought of the only help they could give.

'Bring him out here,' said the minister. 'Our air here is good to a proverb; the June days are fine; he may loiter away his time in the hay-field, and the sweet smells will be a balm in themselves–better than physic.'

'And,' said cousin Holman, scarcely waiting for her husband to finish his sentence, 'tell him there is new milk and fresh eggs to be had for the asking; it's lucky Daisy has just calved, for her milk is always as good as other cows' cream; and there is the plaid room with the morning sun all streaming in.' Phillis said nothing, but looked as much interested in the project as any one. I took it upon myself. I wanted them to see him; him to know them. I proposed it to him when I got home. He was too languid after the day's fatigue, to be willing to make the little exertion of going amongst strangers; and disappointed me by almost declining to accept the invitation I brought. The next morning it was different; he apologized for his ungraciousness of the night before; and told me that he would get all things in train, so as to be ready to go out with me to Hope Farm on the following Saturday.

'For you must go with me, Manning,' said he; 'I used to be as impudent a fellow as need be, and rather liked going amongst strangers, and making my way; but since my illness I am almost like a girl, and turn hot and cold with shyness, as they do, I fancy.'

So it was fixed. We were to go out to Hope Farm on Saturday afternoon; and it was also understood that if the air and the life suited Mr Holdsworth, he was to remain there for a week or ten days, doing what work he could at that end of the line, while I took his place at Eltham to the best of my ability. I grew a little nervous, as the time drew near, and wondered how the brilliant Holdsworth would agree with the quiet quaint family of the minister; how they would like him, and many of his half-foreign ways. I tried to prepare him, by telling him from time to time little things about the goings-on at Hope Farm.

'Manning,' said he, 'I see you don't think I am half good enough for your friends. Out with it, man.'

'No,' I replied, boldly. 'I think you are good; but I don't know if you are quite of their kind of goodness.'

'And you've found out already that there is greater chance of disagreement between two "kinds of goodness", each having its own idea of right, than between a given goodness and a moderate degree of naughtiness–which last often arises from an indifference to right?'

'I don't know. I think you're talking metaphysics, and I am sure that is bad for you.'

'"When a man talks to you in a way that you don't understand about a thing which he does not understand, them's metaphysics." You remember the clown's definition, don't you, Manning?'

'No, I don't,' said I. 'But what I do understand is, that you must go to bed; and tell me at what time we must start tomorrow, that I may go to Hepworth, and get those letters written we were talking about this morning.'

'Wait till to-morrow, and let us see what the day is like,' he answered, with such languid indecision as showed me he was over-fatigued. So I went my way. The morrow was blue and sunny, and beautiful; the very perfection of an early summer's day. Mr Holdsworth was all Impatience to be off into the country; morning had brought back his freshness and strength, and consequent eagerness to be doing. I was afraid we were going to my cousin's farm rather too early, before they would expect us; but what could I do with such a restless vehement man as Holdsworth was that morning? We came down upon the Hope Farm before the dew was off the grass on the shady side of the lane; the great house-dog was loose, basking in the sun, near the closed side door. I was surprised at this door being shut, for all summer long it was open from morning to night; but it was only on latch. I opened it, Rover watching me with half-suspicious, half-trustful eyes. The room was empty.

'I don't know where they can be,' said I. 'But come in and sit down while I go and look for them. You must be tired.'

'Not I. This sweet balmy air is like a thousand tonics. Besides, this room is hot, and smells of those pungent wood-ashes. What are we to do?'

'Go round to the kitchen. Betty will tell us where they are.' So we went round into the farmyard, Rover accompanying us out of a grave sense of duty. Betty was washing out her milk-pans in the cold bubbling spring-water that constantly trickled in and out of a stone trough. In such weather as this most of her kitchen-work was done out of doors.

'Eh, dear!' said she, 'the minister and missus is away at Hornby! They ne'er thought of your coming so betimes! The missus had some errands to do, and she thought as she'd walk with the minister and be back by dinner-time.'

'Did not they expect us to dinner?' said I.

'Well, they did, and they did not, as I may say. Missus said to me the cold lamb would do well enough if you did not come; and if you did I was to put on a chicken and some bacon to boil; and I'll go do it now, for it is hard to boil bacon enough.'

'And is Phillis gone, too?' Mr Holdsworth was making friends with Rover.

'No! She's just somewhere about. I reckon you'll find her in the kitchen-garden, getting peas.

'Let us go there,' said Holsworth, suddenly leaving off his play with the dog. So I led the way into the kitchen-garden. It was in the first promise of a summer profuse in vegetables and fruits. Perhaps it was not so much cared for as other parts of the property; but it was more attended to than most kitchen-gardens belonging to farm-houses. There were borders of flowers along each side of the gravel walks; and there was an old sheltering wail on the north side covered with tolerably choice fruit-trees; there was a slope down to the fish-pond at the end, where there were great strawberry-beds; and raspberry-bushes and rose-bushes grew wherever there was a space; it seemed a chance which had been planted. Long rows of peas stretched at right angles from the main walk, and I saw Phillis stooping down among them, before she saw us. As soon as she heard our cranching steps on the gravel, she stood up, and shading her eyes from the sun, recognized us. She was quite still for a moment, and then came slowly towards us, blushing a little from evident shyness. I had never seen Phillis shy before.

'This is Mr Holdsworth, Phillis,' said I, as soon as I had shaken hands with her. She glanced up at him, and then looked down, more flushed than ever at his grand formality of taking his hat off and bowing; such manners had never been seen at Hope Farm before.

'Father and mother are out. They will be so sorry; you did not write, Paul, as you said you would.'

'It was my fault,' said Holdsworth, understanding what she meant as well as if she had put it more fully into words. 'I have not yet given up all the privileges of an invalid; one of which is indecision. Last night, when your cousin asked me at what time we were to start, I really could not make up my mind.'

Phillis seemed as if she could not make up her mind as to what to do with us. I tried to help her,–

'Have you finished getting peas?' taking hold of the half-filled basket she was unconsciously holding in her hand; 'or may we stay and help you?'

'If you would. But perhaps it will tire you, sir?' added she, speaking now to Holdsworth.

'Not a bit,' said he. 'It will carry me back twenty years in my life, when I used to gather peas in my grandfather's garden. I suppose I may eat a few as I go along?'

'Certainly, sir. But if you went to the strawberry-beds you would find some strawberries ripe, and Paul can show you where they are.'

'I am afraid you distrust me. I can assure you I know the exact fulness at which peas should be gathered. I take great care not to pluck them when they are unripe. I will not be turned off, as unfit for my work.' This was a style of half-joking talk that Phillis was not accustomed to. She looked for a moment as if she would have liked to defend herself from the playful charge of distrust made against her, but she ended by not saying a word. We all plucked our peas in busy silence for the next five minutes. Then Holdsworth lifted himself up from between the rows, and said, a little wearily,

'I am afraid I must strike work. I am not as strong as I fancied myself.' Phillis was full of penitence immediately. He did, indeed, look pale; and she blamed herself for having allowed him to help her.

'It was very thoughtless of me. I did not know—I thought, perhaps, you really liked it. I ought to have offered you something to eat, sir! Oh, Paul, we have gathered quite enough; how stupid I was to forget that Mr Holdsworth had been ill!' And in a blushing hurry she led the way towards the house. We went in, and she moved a heavy cushioned chair forwards, into which Holdsworth was only too glad to sink. Then with deft and quiet speed she brought in a little tray, wine, water, cake, home-made bread, and newly-churned butter. She stood by in some anxiety till, after bite and sup, the colour returned to Mr Holdsworth's face, and he would fain have made us some laughing apologies for the fright he had given us. But then Phillis drew back from her innocent show of care and interest, and relapsed into the cold shyness habitual to her when she was first thrown into the company of strangers. She brought out the last week's county paper (which Mr Holdsworth had read five days ago), and then quietly withdrew; and then he subsided into languor, leaning back and shutting his eyes as if he would go to sleep. I stole into the kitchen after Phillis; but she had made the round of the corner of the house outside, and I found her sitting on the horse-mount, with her basket of peas, and a basin into which she was shelling them. Rover lay at her feet, snapping now and then at the flies. I went to her, and tried to help her, but somehow the sweet crisp young peas found their way more frequently into my mouth than into the basket, while we talked together in a low tone, fearful of being overheard through the open casements of the house-place in which Holdsworth was resting.

'Don't you think him handsome?' asked I.

'Perhaps—yes—I have hardly looked at him,' she replied 'But is not he very like a foreigner?'

'Yes, he cuts his hair foreign fashion,' said I.

'I like an Englishman to look like an Englishman.'

'I don't think he thinks about it. He says he began that way when he was in Italy, because everybody wore it so, and it is natural to keep it on in England.'

'Not if he began it in Italy because everybody there wore it so. Everybody here wears it differently.'

I was a little offended with Phillis's logical fault-finding with my friend; and I determined to change the subject.

'When is your mother coming home?'

'I should think she might come any time now; but she had to go and see Mrs Morton, who was ill, and she might be kept, and not be home till dinner. Don't you think you ought to go and see how Mr Holdsworth is going on, Paul? He may be faint again.'

I went at her bidding; but there was no need for it. Mr Holdsworth was up, standing by the window, his hands in his pockets; he had evidently been watching us. He turned away as I entered.

'So that is the girl I found your good father planning for your wife, Paul, that evening when I interrupted you! Are you of the same coy mind still? It did not look like it a minute ago.'

'Phillis and I understand each other,' I replied, sturdily. 'We are like brother and sister. She would not have me as a husband if there was not another man in the world; and it would take a deal to make me think of her—as my father wishes' (somehow I did not like to say 'as a wife'), 'but we love each other dearly.'

'Well, I am rather surprised at it—not at your loving each other in a brother-and-sister kind of way—but at your finding it so impossible to fall in love with such a beautiful woman.' Woman! beautiful woman! I had thought of Phillis as a comely but awkward girl; and I could not banish the pinafore from my mind's eye when I tried to picture her to myself. Now I turned, as Mr Holdsworth had done, to look at her again out of the window: she had just finished her task, and was standing up, her back to us, holding the basket, and the basin in it, high in air, out of Rover's reach, who was giving vent to his delight at the probability of a change of place by glad leaps and barks, and snatches at what he imagined to be a withheld prize. At length she grew tired of their mutual play, and with a feint of striking him, and a 'Down, Rover! do hush!' she looked towards the window where we were standing, as if to reassure herself that no one had been disturbed by the noise, and seeing us, she coloured all over, and hurried away, with Rover still curving in sinuous lines about her as she walked.

'I should like to have sketched her,' said Mr Holdsworth, as he turned away. He went back to his chair, and rested in silence for a minute or two. Then he was up again.

'I would give a good deal for a book,' he said. 'It would keep me quiet.' He began to look round; there were a few volumes at one end of the shovel-board. 'Fifth volume of Matthew Henry's Commentary,' said he, reading their titles aloud. 'Housewife's complete Manual; Berridge on Prayer; L'Inferno–Dante!' in great surprise. 'Why, who reads this?'

'I told you Phillis read it. Don't you remember? She knows Latin and Greek, too.'

'To be sure! I remember! But somehow I never put two and two together. That quiet girl, full of household work, is the wonderful scholar, then, that put you to rout with her questions when you first began to come here. To be sure, "Cousin Phillis!" What's here: a paper with the hard, obsolete words written out. I wonder what sort of a dictionary she has got. Baretti won't tell her all these words. Stay! I have got a pencil here. I'll write down the most accepted meanings, and save her a little trouble.'

So he took her book and the paper back to the little round table, and employed himself in writing explanations and definitions of the words which had troubled her. I was not sure if he was not taking a liberty: it did not quite please me, and yet I did not know why. He had only just done, and replaced the paper in the book, and put the latter back in its place, when I heard the sound of wheels stopping in the lane, and looking out, I saw cousin Holman getting out of a neighbour's gig, making her little curtsey of acknowledgment, and then coming towards the house. I went to meet her.

'Oh, Paul!' said she, 'I am so sorry I was kept; and then Thomas Dobson said if I would wait a quarter of an hour he would–But where's your friend Mr Holdsworth? I hope he is come?'

Just then he came out, and with his pleasant cordial manner took her hand, and thanked her for asking him to come out here to get strong.

'I'm sure I am very glad to see you, sir. It was the minister's thought. I took it into my head you would be dull in our quiet house, for Paul says you've been such a great traveller; but the minister said that dulness would perhaps suit you while you were but ailing, and that I was to ask Paul to be here as much as he could. I hope you'll find yourself happy with us, I'm sure, sir. Has Phillis given you something to eat and drink, I wonder? there's a deal in eating a little often, if one has to get strong after an illness.' And then she began to question him as to the details of his indisposition in her simple, motherly way. He seemed at once to understand her, and to enter into friendly relations with her. It was not quite the same in the evening when the minister came home. Men have always a little natural antipathy to get over when they first meet as strangers. But in this case each was disposed to make an effort to like the other; only each was to each a specimen of an unknown class. I had to leave the Hope Farm on Sunday afternoon, as I had Mr Holdsworth's work as well as my own to look to in Eltham; and I was not at all sure how things would go on during the week that Holdsworth was to remain on his visit; I had been once or twice in hot water already at the near clash of opinions between the minister and my much-vaunted friend. On the Wednesday I received a short note from Holdsworth; he was going to stay on, and return with me on the following Sunday, and he wanted me to send him a certain list of books, his theodolite, and other surveying instruments, all of which could easily be conveyed down the line to Heathbridge. I went to his lodgings and picked out the books. Italian, Latin, trigonometry;

a pretty considerable parcel they made, besides the implements. I began to be curious as to the general progress of affairs at Hope Farm, but I could not go over till the Saturday. At Heathbridge I found Holdsworth, come to meet me. He was looking quite a different man to what I had left him; embrowned, sparkles in his eyes, so languid before. I told him how much stronger he looked.

'Yes!' said he. 'I am fidging fain to be at work again. Last week I dreaded the thoughts of my employment: now I am full of desire to begin. This week in the country has done wonders for me.'

'You have enjoyed yourself, then?'

'Oh! it has been perfect in its way. Such a thorough country life! and yet removed from the dulness which I always used to fancy accompanied country life, by the extraordinary intelligence of the minister. I have fallen into calling him "the minister"', like every one else.'

'You get on with him, then?' said I. 'I was a little afraid.'

'I was on the verge of displeasing him once or twice, I fear, with random assertions and exaggerated expressions, such as one always uses with other people, and thinks nothing of; but I tried to check myself when I saw how it shocked the good man; and really it is very wholesome exercise, this trying to make one's words represent one's thoughts, instead of merely looking to their effect on others.'

'Then you are quite friends now?' I asked.

'Yes, thoroughly; at any rate as far as I go. I never met with a man with such a desire for knowledge. In information, as far as it can be gained from books, he far exceeds me on most subjects; but then I have travelled and seen—Were not you surprised at the list of things I sent for?'

'Yes; I thought it did not promise much rest.'

'Oh! some of the books were for the minister, and some for his daughter. (I call her Phillis to myself, but I use XX in speaking about her to others. I don't like to seem familiar, and yet Miss Holman is a term I have never heard used.)'

'I thought the Italian books were for her.'

'Yes! Fancy her trying at Dante for her first book in Italian! I had a capital novel by Manzoni, I Promessi Sposi, just the thing for a beginner; and if she must still puzzle out Dante, my dictionary is far better than hers.'

'Then she found out you had written those definitions on her list of words?'

'Oh! yes'–with a smile of amusement and pleasure. He was going to tell me what had taken place, but checked himself.

'But I don't think the minister will like your having given her a novel to read?'

'Pooh! What can be more harmless? Why make a bugbear of a word? It is as pretty and innocent a tale as can be met with. You don't suppose they take Virgil for gospel?'

By this time we were at the farm. I think Phillis gave me a warmer welcome than usual, and cousin Holman was kindness itself. Yet somehow I felt as if I had lost my place, and that Holdsworth had taken it. He knew all the ways of the house; he was full of little filial attentions to cousin Holman; he treated Phillis with the affectionate condescension of an elder brother; not a bit more; not in any way different. He questioned me about the progress of affairs in Eltham with eager interest.

'Ah!' said cousin Holman, 'you'll be spending a different kind of time next week to what you have done this! I can see how busy you'll make yourself! But if you don't take care you'll be ill again, and have to come back to our quiet ways of going on.

'Do you suppose I shall need to be ill to wish to come back here?' he answered, warmly. 'I am only afraid you have treated me so kindly that I shall always be turning up on your hands.'

'That's right,' she replied. 'Only don't go and make yourself ill by over-work. I hope you'll go on with a cup of new milk every morning, for I am sure that is the best medicine; and put a teaspoonful of rum in it, if you like; many a one speaks highly of that, only we had no rum in the house.' I brought with me an atmosphere of active life which I think he had begun to miss; and it was natural that he should seek my company, after his week of retirement. Once I saw Phillis looking at us as we talked together with a kind of wistful curiosity; but as soon as she caught my eye, she turned away, blushing deeply.

That evening I had a little talk with the minister. I strolled along the Hornby road to meet him; for Holdsworth was giving Phillis an Italian lesson, and cousin Holman had fallen asleep over her work. Somehow, and not unwillingly on my part, our talk fell on the friend whom I had introduced to the Hope Farm.

'Yes! I like him!' said the minister, weighing his words a little as he spoke. 'I like him. I hope I am justified in doing it, but he takes hold of me, as it were; and I have almost been afraid lest he carries me away, in spite of my judgment.'

'He is a good fellow; indeed he is,' said I. 'My father thinks well of him; and I have seen a deal of him. I would not have had him come here if I did not know that you would approve of him.'

'Yes,' (once more hesitating,) 'I like him, and I think he is an upright man; there is a want of seriousness in his talk at times, but, at the same time, it is wonderful to listen to him! He makes Horace and Virgil living, instead of dead, by the stories he tells me of his sojourn in the very countries where they lived, and where to this day, he says–But it is like dram-drinking. I listen to him till I forget my duties, and am carried off my feet. Last Sabbath evening he led us away into talk on profane subjects ill befitting the day.' By this time we were at the house, and our conversation stopped. But before the day was out, I saw the unconscious hold that my friend had got over all the family. And no wonder: he had seen so much and done so much as compared to them, and he told about it all so easily and naturally, and yet as I never heard any one else do; and his ready pencil was out in an instant to draw on scraps of paper all sorts of illustrations–modes of drawing up water in Northern Italy, wine-carts, buffaloes, stone-pines, I know not what. After we had all looked at these drawings, Phillis gathered them together, and took them. It is many years since I have seen thee, Edward Holdsworth, but thou wast a delightful fellow! Ay, and a good one too; though much sorrow was caused by thee!

Part III

Just after this I went home for a week's holiday. Everything was prospering there; my father's new partnership gave evident satisfaction to both parties. There was no display of increased wealth in our modest household; but my mother had a few extra comforts provided for her by her husband. I made acquaintance with Mr and Mrs Ellison, and first saw pretty Margaret Ellison, who is now my wife. When I returned to Eltham, I found that a step was decided upon, which had been in contemplation for some time; that Holdsworth and I should remove our quarters to Hornby; our daily presence, and as much of our time as possible, being required for the completion of the line at that end.

Of course this led to greater facility of intercourse with the Hope Farm people. We could easily walk out there after our day's work was done, and spend a balmy evening hour or two, and yet return before the summer's twilight had quite faded away. Many a time, indeed, we would fain have stayed longer–the open air, the fresh and pleasant country, made so agreeable a contrast to the close, hot town lodgings which I shared with Mr Holdsworth; but early hours, both at eve and morn, were an imperative necessity with the minister, and he made no scruple at turning either or both of us out of the house directly after evening prayer, or 'exercise', as he called it. The remembrance of many a happy day, and of several little scenes, comes back upon me as I think of that summer. They rise like pictures to my memory, and in this way I can date their succession; for I know that corn harvest must have come after hay-making, apple-gathering after corn-harvest.

The removal to Hornby took up some time, during which we had neither of us any leisure to go out to the Hope Farm. Mr Holdsworth had been out there once during my absence at home. One sultry evening, when work was done, he proposed our walking out and paying the Holmans a visit. It so happened that I had omitted to write my usual weekly letter home in our press of business, and I wished to finish that before going out. Then he said that he would go, and that I could follow him if I liked. This I did in about an hour; the weather was so oppressive, I remember, that I took off my coat as I walked, and hung it over my arm. All the doors and windows at the farm were open when I arrived there, and every tiny leaf on the trees was still. The silence of the place was profound; at first I thought that it was entirely deserted; but just as I drew near the door I heard a weak sweet voice begin to sing; it was cousin Holman, all by herself in the house-place, piping up a hymn, as she knitted away in the clouded light. She gave me a kindly welcome, and poured out all the small domestic news of the fortnight past upon me, and, in return, I told her about my own people and my visit at home.

'Where were the rest?' at length I asked.

Betty and the men were in the field helping with the last load of hay, for the minister said there would be rain before the morning. Yes, and the minister himself, and Phillis, and Mr Holdsworth, were all there helping. She thought that she herself could have done something; but perhaps she was the least fit for hay-making of any one; and somebody must stay at home and take care of the house, there were so many tramps about; if I had not had something to do with the railroad she would have called them navvies. I asked her if she minded being left alone, as I should like to go arid help; and having her full and glad permission to leave her alone, I went off, following her directions: through the farmyard, past the cattle-pond, into the ashfield, beyond into the higher field with two holly-bushes in the middle. I arrived there: there was Betty with all the farming men, and a cleared field, and a heavily laden cart; one man at the top of the great pile ready to catch the fragrant hay which the others threw up to him with their pitchforks; a little heap of cast-off clothes in a corner of the field (for the heat, even at seven o'clock, was insufferable), a few cans and baskets, and Rover lying by them panting, and keeping watch. Plenty of loud, hearty, cheerful talking; but no minister, no Phillis, no Mr Holdsworth. Betty saw me first, and understanding who it was that I was in search of, she came towards me.

'They're out yonder–agait wi' them things o' Measter Holdsworth's.' So 'out yonder' I went; out on to a broad upland common, full of red sand-banks, and sweeps and hollows; bordered by dark firs, purple in the coming shadows, but near at hand all ablaze with flowering gorse, or, as we call it in the south, furze-bushes, which, seen against the belt of distant trees, appeared brilliantly golden. On this heath, a little way from the field-gate, I saw the three. I counted their heads, joined together in an eager group over Holdsworth's theodolite. He was teaching the minister the practical art of surveying and taking a level. I was wanted to assist, and was quickly set to work to hold the chain. Phillis was as intent as her father; she had hardly time to greet me, so desirous was she to hear some answer to her father's question. So we went on, the dark clouds still gathering, for perhaps five minutes after my arrival. Then came the blinding lightning and the rumble and quick-following rattling peal of thunder right over our heads. It came sooner than I expected, sooner than they had looked for: the rain delayed not; it came pouring down; and what were we to do for shelter? Philiis had nothing on but her indoor things–no bonnet, no shawl. Quick as the darting lightning around us, Holdsworth took off his coat and wrapped it round her neck and shoulders, and, almost without a word, hurried us all into such poor shelter as one of the overhanging sand-banks could give. There we were, cowered down, close together, Phillis innermost, almost too tightly packed to free her arms enough to divest herself of the coat, which she, in her turn, tried to put lightly over Holdsworth's shoulders. In doing so she touched his shirt.

'Oh, how wet you are!' she cried, in pitying dismay; 'and you've hardly got over your fever! Oh, Mr Holdsworth, I am so sorry!' He turned his head a little, smiling at her.

'If I do catch cold, it is all my fault for having deluded you into staying out here!' but she only murmured again, 'I am so sorry.' The minister spoke now. 'It is a regular downpour. Please God that the hay is saved! But there is no likelihood of its ceasing, and I had better go home at once, and send you all some wraps; umbrellas will not be safe with yonder thunder and lightning.'

Both Holdsworth and I offered to go instead of him; but he was resolved, although perhaps it would have been wiser if Holdsworth, wet as he already was, had kept himself in exercise. As he moved off, Phillis crept out, and could see on to the storm-swept heath. Part of Holdsworth's apparatus still remained exposed to all the rain. Before we could have any warning, she had rushed out of the shelter and collected the various things, and brought them back in triumph to where we crouched. Holdsworth had stood up, uncertain whether to go to her assistance or not. She came running back, her long lovely hair floating and dripping, her eyes glad and bright, and her colour freshened to a glow of health by the exercise and the rain.

'Now, Miss Holman, that's what I call wilful,' said Holdsworth, as she gave them to him. 'No, I won't thank you' (his looks were thanking her all the time). 'My little bit of dampness annoyed you, because you thought I had got wet in your service; so you were determined to make me as uncomfortable as you were yourself. It was an unchristian piece of revenge!'

His tone of badinage (as the French call it) would have been palpable enough to any one accustomed to the world; but Phillis was not, and it distressed or rather bewildered her. 'Unchristian' had to her a very serious meaning; it was not a word to be used lightly; and though she did not exactly understand what wrong it was that she was accused of doing, she was evidently desirous to throw off the imputation. At first her earnestness to disclaim unkind motives amused Holdsworth; while his light continuance of the joke perplexed her still more; but at last he said something gravely, and in too low a tone for me to hear, which made her all at once become silent, and called out her blushes. After a while, the minister came back, a moving mass of shawls, cloaks, and umbrellas. Phillis kept very close to her father's side on our return to the farm. She appeared to me to be shrinking away from Holdsworth, while he had not the slightest variation in his manner from what it usually was in his graver moods; kind, protecting, and thoughtful towards her. Of course, there was a great commotion about our wet clothes; but I name the little events of that evening now because I wondered at the time what he had said in that low voice to silence Phillis so effectually, and because, in thinking of their intercourse by the light of future events, that evening stands out with some prominence. I have said that after our removal to Hornby our communications with the farm became almost of daily occurrence. Cousin Holman and I were the two who had least to do with this intimacy. After Mr Holdsworth regained his health, he too often talked above her head in intellectual matters, and too often in his light bantering tone for her to feel quite at her ease with him. I really believe that he adopted this latter tone in speaking to her because he did not know what to talk about to a purely motherly woman, whose intellect had never been cultivated, and whose loving heart was entirely occupied with her husband, her child, her household affairs and, perhaps, a little with the concerns of the members of her husband's congregation, because they, in a way, belonged to her husband. I had noticed before that she had fleeting shadows of jealousy even of Phillis, when her daughter and her husband appeared to have strong interests and sympathies in things which were quite beyond her comprehension. I had noticed it in my first acquaintance with them, I say, and had admired the delicate tact which made the minister, on such occasions, bring the conversation back to such subjects as those on which his wife, with her practical experience of every-day life, was an authority; while Phillis, devoted to her father, unconsciously followed his lead, totally unaware, in her filial reverence, of his motive for doing so.

To return to Holdsworth. The minister had at more than one time spoken of him to me with slight distrust, principally occasioned by the suspicion that his careless words were not always those of soberness and truth. But it was more as a protest against the fascination which the younger man evidently exercised over the elder one more as it were to strengthen himself against yielding to this fascination–that the minister spoke out to me about this failing of Holdsworth's, as it appeared to him. In return Holdsworth was subdued by the minister's uprightness and goodness, and delighted with his clear intellect–his strong healthy craving after further knowledge. I never met two men who took more thorough pleasure and relish in each other's society. To Phillis his relation continued that of an elder brother: he directed her studies into new paths, he patiently drew out the expression of many of her thoughts, and perplexities, and unformed theories–scarcely ever now falling into the vein of banter which she was so slow to understand.

One day–harvest-time–he had been drawing on a loose piece of paper-sketching ears of corn, sketching carts drawn by bullocks and laden with grapes–all the time talking with Phillis and me, cousin Holman putting in her not pertinent remarks, when suddenly he said to Phillis,–

'Keep your head still; I see a sketch! I have often tried to draw your head from memory, and failed; but I think I can do it now. If I succeed I will give it to your mother. You would like a portrait of your daughter as Ceres, would you not, ma'am?'

'I should like a picture of her; yes, very much, thank you, Mr Holdsworth; but if you put that straw in her hair,' (he was holding some wheat ears above her passive head, looking at the effect with an artistic eye,) 'you'll ruffle her hair. Phillis, my dear, if you're to have your picture taken, go up-stairs, and brush your hair smooth.'

'Not on any account. I beg your pardon, but I want hair loosely flowing.' He began to draw, looking intently at Phillis; I could see this stare of his discomposed her–her colour came and went, her breath quickened with the consciousness of his regard; at last, when he said, 'Please look at me for a minute or two, I want to get in the eyes,' she looked up at him, quivered, and suddenly got up and left the room. He did not say a word, but went on with some other part of the drawing; his silence was unnatural, and his dark cheek blanched a little. Cousin Holman looked up from her work, and put her spectacles down.

'What's the matter? Where is she gone?'

Holdsworth never uttered a word, but went on drawing. I felt obliged to say something; it was stupid enough, but stupidity was better than silence just then.

'I'll go and call her,' said I. So I went into the hall, and to the bottom of the stairs; but just as I was going to call Phillis, she came down swiftly with her bonnet on, and saying, 'I'm going to father in the five-acre,' passed out by the open 'rector,' right in front of the house-place windows, and out at the little white side-gate. She had been seen by her mother and Holdsworth, as she passed; so there was no need for explanation, only cousin Holman and I had a long discussion as to whether she could have found the room too hot, or what had occasioned her sudden departure. Holdsworth was very quiet during all the rest of that day; nor did he resume the portrait-taking by his own desire, only at my cousin Holman's request the next time that he came; and then he said he should not require any more formal sittings for only such a slight sketch as he felt himself capable of making. Phillis was just the same as ever the next time I saw her after her abrupt passing me in the hall. She never gave any explanation of her rush out of the room.

So all things went on, at least as far as my observation reached at the time, or memory can recall now, till the great apple-gathering of the year. The nights were frosty, the mornings and evenings were misty, but at mid-day all was sunny and bright, and it was one mid-day that both of us being on the line near Heathbridge, and knowing that they were gathering apples at the farm, we resolved to spend the men's dinner-hour in going over there. We found the great clothes-baskets full of apples, scenting the house, and stopping up the way; and an universal air of merry contentment with this the final produce of the year. The yellow leaves hung on the trees ready to flutter down at the slightest puff of air; the great bushes of Michaelmas daisies in the kitchen-garden were making their last show of flowers. We must needs taste the fruit off the different trees, and pass our judgment as to their flavour; and we went away with our pockets stuffed with those that we liked best. As we had passed to the orchard, Holdsworth had admired and spoken about some flower which he saw; it so happened he had never seen this old-fashioned kind since the days of his boyhood. I do not know whether he had thought anything more about this chance speech of his, but I know I had not—when Phillis, who had been missing just at the last moment of our hurried visit, re-appeared with a little nosegay of this same flower, which she was tying up with a blade of grass. She offered it to Holdsworth as he stood with her father on the point of departure. I saw their faces. I saw for the first time an unmistakable look of love in his black eyes; it was more than gratitude for the little attention; it was tender and beseeching—passionate. She shrank from it in confusion, her glance fell on me; and, partly to hide her emotion, partly out of real kindness at what might appear ungracious neglect of an older friend, she flew off to gather me a few late-blooming China roses. But it was the first time she had ever done anything of the kind for me.

We had to walk fast to be back on the line before the men's return, so we spoke but little to each other, and of course the afternoon was too much occupied for us to have any talk. In the evening we went back to our joint lodgings in Hornby. There, on the table, lay a letter for

Holdsworth, which had be en forwarded to him from Eltham. As our tea was ready, and I had had nothing to eat since morning, I fell to directly without paying much attention to my companion as he opened and read his letter. He was very silent for a few minutes; at length he said,

'Old fellow! I'm going to leave you!'

'Leave me!' said I. 'How? When?'

'This letter ought to have come to hand Sooner. It is from Greathed the engineer' (Greathed was well known in those days; he is dead now, and his name half-forgotten); 'he wants to see me about Some business; in fact, I may as well tell you, Paul, this letter contains a very advantageous proposal for me to go out to Canada, and superintend the making of a line there.' I was in utter dismay. 'But what will Our company say to that?' 'Oh, Greathed has the superintendence of this line, you know; and he is going to be engineer in chief to this Canadian line; many of the Shareholders in this company are going in for the other, so I fancy they will make no difficulty in following Greathed's lead. He says he has a young man ready to put in my place.'

'I hate him,' said I.

'Thank you,' said Holdsworth, laughing.

'But you must not,' he resumed; 'for this is a very good thing for me, and, of course, if no one can be found to take my inferior work, I can't be spared to take the superior. I only wish I had received this letter a day Sooner. Every hour is of consequence, for Greathed says they are threatening a rival line. Do you know, Paul, I almost fancy I must go up tonight? I can take an engine back to Eltham, and catch the night train. I should not like Greathed to think me luke-warm.'

'But you'll come back?' I asked, distressed at the thought of this sudden parting.

'Oh, yes! At least I hope so. They may want me to go out by the next steamer, that will be on Saturday.' He began to eat and drink standing, but I think he was quite unconscious of the nature of either his food or his drink.

'I will go to-night. Activity and readiness go a long way in our profession. Remember that, my boy! I hope I shall come back, but if I don't, be sure and recollect all the words of wisdom that have fallen from my lips. Now where's the portmanteau? If I can gain half an hour for a gathering up of my things in Eltham, so much the better. I'm clear of debt anyhow; and what I owe for my lodgings you can pay for me out of my quarter's salary, due November 4th.'

'Then you don't think you will come back?' I said, despondingly.

'I will come back some time, never fear,' said he, kindly. 'I may be back in a couple of days, having been found in-competent for the Canadian work; or I may not be wanted to go out so soon as I now anticipate. Anyhow you don't suppose I am going to forget you, Paul this work out there ought not to take me above two years, and, perhaps, after that, we may be employed together again.' Perhaps! I had very little hope. The same kind of happy days never returns. However, I did all I could in helping him: clothes, papers, books, instruments; how we pushed and struggled—how I stuffed. All was done in a much shorter time than we had calculated upon, when I had run down to the sheds to order the engine. I was going to drive him to Eltham. We sate ready for a summons. Holdsworth took up the little nosegay that he had brought away from the Hope Farm, and had laid on the mantel-piece on first coming into the room. He smelt at it, and caressed it with his lips.

'What grieves me is that I did not know—that I have not said good-bye to—to them.'

He spoke in a grave tone, the shadow of the coming separation falling upon him at last.

'I will tell them,' said I. 'I am sure they will be very sorry.' Then we were silent.

'I never liked any family so much.'

'I knew you would like them.'

'How one's thoughts change,—this morning I was full of a hope, Paul.' He paused, and then he said,—

'You put that sketch in carefully?'

'That outline of a head?' asked I. But I knew he meant an abortive sketch of Phillis, which had not been successful enough for him to complete it with shading or colouring.

'Yes. What a sweet innocent face it is! and yet so—Oh, dear!' He sighed and got up, his hands in his pockets, to walk up and down the room in evident disturbance of mind. He suddenly stopped opposite to me.

'You'll tell them how it all was. Be sure and tell the good minister that I was so sorry not to wish him good-bye, and to thank him and his wife for all their kindness. As for Phillis,–please God in two years I'll be back and tell her myself all in my heart.'

'You love Phillis, then?' said I.

'Love her! Yes, that I do. Who could help it, seeing her as I have done? Her character as unusual and rare as her beauty! God bless her! God keep her in her high tranquillity, her pure innocence.–Two years! It is a long time.–But she lives in such seclusion, almost like the sleeping beauty, Paul,'–(he was smiling now, though a minute before I had thought him on the verge of tears,) –'but I shall come back like a prince from Canada, and waken her to my love. I can't help hoping that it won't be difficult, eh, Paul?'

This touch of coxcombry displeased me a little, and I made no answer. He went on, half apologetically,–

'You see, the salary they offer me is large; and beside that, this experience will give me a name which will entitle me to expect a still larger in any future undertaking.'

'That won't influence Phillis.'

'No! but it will make me more eligible in the eyes of her father and mother.' I made no answer.

'You give me your best wishes, Paul,' said he, almost pleading. 'You would like me for a cousin?'

I heard the scream and whistle of the engine ready down at the sheds.

'Ay, that I should,' I replied, suddenly softened towards my friend now that he was going away. 'I wish you were to be married to-morrow, and I were to be best man.'

'Thank you, lad. Now for this cursed portmanteau (how the minister would be shocked); but it is heavy!' and off we sped into the darkness. He only just caught the night train at Eltham, and I slept, desolately enough, at my old lodgings at Miss Dawsons', for that night. Of course the next few days I was busier than ever, doing both his work and my own. Then came a letter from him, very short and affectionate. He was going out in the Saturday steamer, as he had more than half expected;

and by the following Monday the man who was to succeed him would
be down at Eltham. There was a P.S., with only these words:– 'My
nosegay goes with me to Canada, but I do not need it to remind me of
Hope Farm.'

Saturday came; but it was very late before I could go out to the farm.
It was a frosty night, the stars shone clear above me, and the road was
crisping beneath my feet. They must have heard my footsteps before I
got up to the house. They were sitting at their usual employments in the
house-place when I went in. Phillis's eyes went beyond me in their
look of welcome, and then fell in quiet disappointment on her work.

'And where's Mr Holdsworth?' asked cousin Holman, in a minute
or two. 'I hope his cold is not worse,–I did not like his short cough.'

I laughed awkwardly; for I felt that I was the bearer of unpleasant
news.

'His cold had need be better–for he's gone–gone away to Canada!'

I purposely looked away from Phillis, as I thus abruptly told my
news.

'To Canada!' said the minister.

'Gone away!' said his wife. But no word from Phillis.

'Yes!' said I. 'He found a letter at Hornby when we got home the
other night– when we got home from here; he ought to have got it
sooner; he was ordered to go up to London directly, and to see some
people about a new line in Canada, and he's gone to lay it down; he has
sailed to-day. He was sadly grieved not to have time to come out and
wish you all good-by; but he started for London within two hours after
he got that letter. He bade me thank you most gratefully for all your
kindnesses; he was very sorry not to come here once again.' Phillis got
up and left the room with noiseless steps.

'I am very sorry,' said the minister.

'I am sure so am I!' said cousin Holman. 'I was real fond of that lad
ever since I nursed him last June after that bad fever.'

The minister went on asking me questions respecting Holdsworth's
future plans; and brought out a large old-fashioned atlas, that he might
find out the exact places between which the new railroad was to run.
Then supper was ready; it was always on the table as soon as the clock
on the stairs struck eight, and down came Phillis–her face white and

set, her dry eyes looking defiance to me, for I am afraid I hurt her maidenly pride by my glance of sympathetic interest as she entered the room. Never a word did she say–never a question did she ask about the absent friend, yet she forced herself to talk.

And so it was all the next day. She was as pale as could be, like one who has received some shock; but she would not let me talk to her, and she tried hard to behave as usual. Two or three times I repeated, in public, the various affectionate messages to the family with which I was charged by Holdsworth; but she took no more notice of them than if my words had been empty air. And in this mood I left her on the Sabbath evening.

My new master was not half so indulgent as my old one. He kept up strict discipline as to hours, so that it was some time before I could again go out, even to pay a call at the Hope Farm.

It was a cold misty evening in November. The air, even indoors, seemed full of haze; yet there was a great log burning on the hearth, which ought to have made the room cheerful. Cousin Holman and Phillis were sitting at the little round table before the fire, working away in silence. The minister had his books out on the dresser, seemingly deep in study, by the light of his solitary candle; perhaps the fear of disturbing him made the unusual stillness of the room. But a welcome was ready for me from all; not noisy, not demonstrative–that it never was; my damp wrappers were taken off; the next meal was hastened, and a chair placed for me on one side of the fire, so that I pretty much commanded a view of the room. My eye caught on Phillis, looking so pale and weary, and with a sort of aching tone (if I may call it so) in her voice. She was doing all the accustomed things–fulfilling small household duties, but somehow differently–I can't tell you how, for she was just as deft and quick in her movements, only the light spring was gone out of them. Cousin Holman began to question me; even the minister put aside his books, and came and stood on the opposite side of the fire-place, to hear what waft of intelligence I brought. I had first to tell them why I had not been to see them for so long–more than five weeks. The answer was simple enough; business and the necessity of attending strictly to the orders of a new superintendent, who had not yet learned trust, much less indulgence.

The minister nodded his approval of my conduct, and said,– 'Right, Paul! "Servants, obey in all things your master according to the flesh." I have had my fears lest you had too much licence under Edward Holdsworth.'

'Ah,' said cousin Holman, 'poor Mr Holdsworth, he'll be on the salt seas by this time!'

'No, indeed,' said I, 'he's landed. I have had a letter from him from Halifax.' Immediately a shower of questions fell thick upon me. When? How? What was he doing? How did he like it? What sort of a voyage? &c.

'Many is the time we have thought of him when the wind was blowing so hard; the old quince-tree is blown down, Paul, that on the right-hand of the great pear-tree; it was blown down last Monday week, and it was that night that I asked the minister to pray in an especial manner for all them that went down in ships upon the great deep, and he said then, that Mr Holdsworth might be already landed; but I said, even if the prayer did not fit him, it was sure to be fitting somebody out at sea, who would need the Lord's care. Both Phillis and I thought he would be a month on the seas.' Phillis began to speak, but her voice did not come rightly at first. It was a little higher pitched than usual, when she said,–

'We thought he would be a month if he went in a sailing-vessel, or perhaps longer. I suppose he went in a steamer?'

'Old Obadiah Grimshaw was more than six weeks in getting to America,' observed cousin Holman.

'I presume he cannot as yet tell how he likes his new work?' asked the minister.

'No! he is but just landed; it is but one page long. I'll read it to you, shall I?–

'"Dear Paul,–We are safe on shore, after a rough passage. Thought you would like to hear this, but homeward-bound steamer is making signals for letters. Will write again soon. It seems a year since I left Hornby. Longer since I was at the farm. I have got my nosegay safe. Remember me to the Holmans.–Yours, E. H."'

'That's not much, certainly,' said the minister. 'But it's a comfort to know he's on land these blowy nights.'

Phillis said nothing. She kept her head bent down over her work; but I don't think she put a stitch in, while I was reading the letter. I wondered if she understood what nosegay was meant; but I could not tell. When next she lifted up her face, there were two spots of brilliant colour on the cheeks that had been so pale before. After I had spent an hour or two there, I was bound to return back to Hornby. I told them I did not know when I could come again, as we–by which I mean the company–had undertaken the Hensleydale line; that branch for which poor Holdsworth was surveying when he caught his fever.

'But you'll have a holiday at Christmas,' said my cousin. 'Surely they'll not be such heathens as to work you then?'

'Perhaps the lad will be going home,' said the minister, as if to mitigate his wife's urgency; but for all that, I believe he wanted me to come. Phillis fixed her eyes on me with a wistful expression, hard to resist. But, indeed, I had no thought of resisting. Under my new master I had no hope of a holiday long enough to enable me to go to Birmingham and see my parents with any comfort; and nothing could be pleasanter to me than to find myself at home at my cousins' for a day or two, then. So it was fixed that we were to meet in Hornby Chapel on Christmas Day, and that I was to accompany them home after service, and if possible to stay over the next day.

I was not able to get to chapel till late on the appointed day, and so I took a seat near the door in considerable shame, although it really was not my fault. When the service was ended, I went and stood in the porch to await the coming out of my cousins. Some worthy people belonging to the congregation clustered into a group just where I stood, and exchanged the good wishes of the season. It had just begun to snow, and this occasioned a little delay, and they fell into further conversation. I was not attending to what was not meant for me to hear, till I caught the name of Phillis Holman. And then I listened; where was the harm?

'I never saw any one so changed!'

'I asked Mrs Holman,' quoth another, '"Is Phillis well?" and she just said she had been having a cold which had pulled her down; she did not seem to think anything of it.'

'They had best take care of her,' said one of the oldest of the good ladies; 'Phillis comes of a family as is not long-lived. Her mother's sister, Lydia Green, her own aunt as was, died of a decline just when she was about this lass's age.'

This ill-omened talk was broken in upon by the coming out of the minister, his wife and daughter, and the consequent interchange of Christmas compliments. I had had a shock, and felt heavy-hearted and anxious, and hardly up to making the appropriate replies to the kind greetings of my relations. I looked askance at Phillis. She had certainly grown taller and slighter, and was thinner; but there was a flush of colour on her face which deceived me for a time, and made me think she was looking as well as ever. I only saw her paleness after we had returned to the farm, and she had subsided into silence and quiet. Her grey eyes looked hollow and sad; her complexion was of a dead white. But she went about just as usual; at least, just as she had done the last time I was there, and seemed to have no ailment; and I was inclined to think that my cousin was right when she had answered the inquiries of the good-natured gossips, and told them that Phillis was suffering from the consequences of a bad cold, nothing more. I have said that I was to stay over the next day; a great deal of snow had come down, but not all, they said, though the ground was covered deep with the white fall. The minister was anxiously housing his cattle, and preparing all things for a long continuance of the same kind of weather. The men were chopping wood, sending wheat to the mill to be ground before the road should become impassable for a cart and horse. My cousin and Phillis had gone up-stairs to the apple-room to cover up the fruit from the frost. I had been out the greater part of the morning, and came in about an hour before dinner. To my surprise, knowing how she had planned to be engaged, I found Phillis sitting at the dresser, resting her head on her two hands and reading, or seeming to read. She did not look up when I came in, but murmured something about her mother having sent her down out of the cold. It flashed across me that she was crying, but I put it down to some little spirt of temper; I might have known better than to suspect the gentle, serene Phillis of crossness, poor girl; I stooped down, and began to stir and build up the fire, which appeared to have been neglected. While my head was down I heard a noise which made me pause and listen–a sob, an unmistakable, irrepressible sob. I started up.

'Phillis!' I cried, going towards her, with my hand out, to take hers for sympathy with her sorrow, whatever it was. But she was too quick for me, she held her hand out of my grasp, for fear of my detaining her; as she quickly passed out of the house, she said,–

'Don't, Paul! I cannot bear it!' and passed me, still sobbing, and went out into the keen, open air.

I stood still and wondered. What could have come to Phillis? The most perfect harmony prevailed in the family, and Phillis especially, good and gentle as she was, was so beloved that if they had found out that her finger ached, it would have cast a shadow over their hearts. Had I done anything to vex her? No: she was crying before I came in. I went to look at her book–one of those unintelligible Italian books. I could make neither head nor tail of it. I saw some pencil-notes on the margin, in Holdsworth's handwriting.

Could that be it? Could that be the cause of her white looks, her weary eyes, her wasted figure, her struggling sobs? This idea came upon me like a flash of lightning on a dark night, making all things so clear we cannot forget them afterwards when the gloomy obscurity returns. I was still standing with the book in my hand when I heard cousin Holman's footsteps on the stairs, and as I did not wish to speak to her just then, I followed Phillis's example, and rushed out of the house. The snow was lying on the ground; I could track her feet by the marks they had made; I could see where Rover had joined her. I followed on till I came to a great stack of wood in the orchard–it was built up against the back wall of the outbuildings,–and I recollected then how Phillis had told me, that first day when we strolled about together, that underneath this stack had been her hermitage, her sanctuary, when she was a child; how she used to bring her book to study there, or her work, when she was not wanted in the house; and she had now evidently gone back to this quiet retreat of her childhood, forgetful of the clue given me by her footmarks on the new-fallen snow. The stack was built up very high; but through the interstices of the sticks I could see her figure, although I did not all at once perceive how I could get to her. She was sitting on a log of wood, Rover by her.

She had laid her cheek on Rover's head, and had her arm round his neck, partly for a pillow, partly from an instinctive craving for warmth on that bitter cold day. She was making a low moan, like an animal in pain, or perhaps more like the sobbing of the wind. Rover, highly flattered by her caress, and also, perhaps, touched by sympathy, was flapping his heavy tail against the ground, but not otherwise moving a hair, until he heard my approach with his quick erected ears. Then, with a short, abrupt bark of distrust, he sprang up as if to leave his mistress. Both he and I were immovably still for a moment. I was not sure if what I longed to do was wise: and yet I could not bear to see the sweet serenity of my dear cousin's life so disturbed by a suffering which I thought I could assuage. But Rover's ears were sharper than my breathing was noiseless: he heard me, and sprang out from under Phillis's restraining hand.

'Oh, Rover, don't you leave me, too,' she plained out.

'Phillis!' said I, seeing by Rover's exit that the entrance to where she sate was to be found on the other side of the stack. 'Phillis, come out! You have got a cold already; and it is not fit for you to sit there on such a day as this. You know how displeased and anxious it would make them all.'

She sighed, but obeyed; stooping a little, she came out, and stood upright, opposite to me in the lonely, leafless orchard. Her face looked so meek and so sad that I felt as if I ought to beg her pardon for my necessarily authoritative words.

'Sometimes I feel the house so close,' she said; 'and I used to sit under the wood-stack when I was a child. It was very kind of you, but there was no need to come after me. I don't catch cold easily.'

'Come with me into this cow-house, Phillis. I have got something to say to you; and I can't stand this cold, if you can.

I think she would have fain run away again; but her fit of energy was all spent. She followed me unwillingly enough that I could see. The place to which I took her was full of the fragrant breath of the cows, and was a little warmer than the outer air. I put her inside, and stood myself in the doorway, thinking how I could best begin. At last I plunged into it.

'I must see that you don't get cold for more reasons than one; if you are ill, Holdsworth will be so anxious and miserable out there' (by which I meant Canada)–

She shot one penetrating look at me, and then turned her face away with a slightly impatient movement. If she could have run away then she would, but I held the means of exit in my own power. 'In for a penny, in for a pound,' thought I, and I went on rapidly, anyhow.

'He talked so much about you, just before he left–that night after he had been here, you know–and you had given him those flowers.' She put her hands up to hide her face, but she was listening now–listening with all her ears. 'He had never spoken much about you before, but the sudden going away unlocked his heart, and he told me how he loved you, and how he hoped on his return that you might be his wife.'

'Don't,' said she, almost gasping out the word, which she had tried once or twice before to speak; but her voice had been choked. Now she put her hand backwards; she had quite turned away from me, and felt for mine. She gave it a soft lingering pressure; and then she put her arms down on the wooden division, and laid her head on it, and cried quiet tears. I did not understand her at once, and feared lest I had mistaken the whole case, and only annoyed her. I went up to her. 'Oh, Phillis! I am so sorry–I thought you would, perhaps, have cared to hear it; he did talk so feelingly, as if he did love you so much, and somehow I thought it would give you pleasure.'

She lifted up her head and looked at me. Such a look! Her eyes, glittering with tears as they were, expressed an almost heavenly happiness; her tender mouth was curved with rapture–her colour vivid and blushing; but as if she was afraid her face expressed too much, more than the thankfulness to me she was essaying to speak, she hid it again almost immediately. So it was all right then, and my conjecture was well-founded! I tried to remember something more to tell her of what he had said, but again she stopped me.

'Don't,' she said. She still kept her face covered and hidden. In half a minute she added, in a very low voice, 'Please, Paul, I think I would rather not hear any more I don't mean but what I have–but what I am very much obliged–Only–only, I think I would rather hear the rest from himself when he comes back.'

And then she cried a little more, in quite a different way. I did not say any more, I waited for her. By-and-by she turned towards me—not meeting my eyes, however; and putting her hand in mine just as if we were two children, she said,—

'We had best go back now—I don't look as if I had been crying, do I?'

'You look as if you had a bad cold,' was all the answer I made.

'Oh! but I am quite well, only cold; and a good run will warm me. Come along, Paul.'

So we ran, hand in hand, till, just as we were on the threshold of the house, she stopped,—

'Paul, please, we won't speak about that again.'

Part IV

When I went over on Easter Day I heard the chapel-gossips complimenting cousin Holman on her daughter's blooming looks, quite forgetful of their sinister prophecies three months before. And I looked at Phillis, and did not wonder at their words. I had not seen her since the day after Christmas Day. I had left the Hope Farm only a few hours after I had told her the news which had quickened her heart into renewed life and vigour. The remembrance of our conversation in the cow-house was vividly in my mind as I looked at her when her bright healthy appearance was remarked upon. As her eyes met mine our mutual recollections flashed intelligence from one to the other. She turned away, her colour heightening as she did so. She seemed to be shy of me for the first few hours after our meeting, and I felt rather vexed with her for her conscious avoidance of me after my long absence. I had stepped a little out of my usual line in telling her what I did; not that I had received any charge of secrecy, or given even the slightest promise to Holdsworth that I would not repeat his words. But I had an uneasy feeling sometimes when I thought of what I had done in the excitement of seeing Phillis so ill and in so much trouble. I meant to have told Holdsworth when I wrote next to him; but when I had my half-finished letter before me I sate with my pen in my hand hesitating. I had more scruple in revealing what I had found out or guessed at of Phillis's secret than in repeating to her his spoken words. I did not think I had any right to say out to him what I believed–namely, that she loved him dearly, and had felt his absence even to the injury of her health. Yet to explain what I had done in telling her how he had spoken about her that last night, it would be necessary to give my reasons, so I had settled within myself to leave it alone. As she had told me she should like to hear all the details and fuller particulars and more explicit declarations first from him, so he should have the pleasure of extracting the delicious tender secret from her maidenly lips. I would not betray my guesses, my surmises, my all but certain knowledge of the state of her heart. I had received two letters from him after he had settled to his business; they were full of

life and energy; but in each there had been a message to the family at
the Hope Farm of more than common regard; and a slight but distinct
mention of Phillis herself, showing that she stood single and alone in
his memory. These letters I had sent on to the minister, for he was sure
to care for them, even supposing he had been unacquainted with their
writer, because they were so clever and so picturesquely worded that
they brought, as it were, a whiff of foreign atmosphere into his
circumscribed life. I used to wonder what was the trade or business in
which the minister would not have thriven, mentally I mean, if it had
so happened that he had been called into that state. He would have
made a capital engineer, that I know; and he had a fancy for the sea,
like many other land-locked men to whom the great deep is a mystery
and a fascination. He read law-books with relish; and, once happening
to borrow De Lolme on the British Constitution (or some such title), he
talked about jurisprudence till he was far beyond my depth. But to
return to Holdsworth's letters. When the minister sent them back he
also wrote out a list of questions suggested by their perusal, which I
was to pass on in my answers to Holdsworth, until I thought of
suggesting direct correspondence between the two. That was the state
of things as regarded the absent one when I went to the farm for my
Easter visit, and when I found Phillis in that state of shy reserve
towards me which I have named before. I thought she was ungrateful;
for I was not quite sure if I had done wisely in having told her what I
did. I had committed a fault, or a folly, perhaps, and all for her sake;
and here was she, less friends with me than she had even been before.
This little estrangement only lasted a few hours. I think that as Soon as
she felt pretty sure of there being no recurrence, either by word, look,
or allusion, to the one subject that was predominant in her mind, she
came back to her old sisterly ways with me. She had much to tell me
of her own familiar interests; how Rover had been ill, and how anxious
they had all of them been, and how, after some little discussion
between her father and her, both equally grieved by the sufferings of
the old dog, he had been remembered in the household prayers', and
how he had begun to get better only the very next day, and then she
would have led me into a conversation on the right ends of prayer, and
on special providences, and I know not what; only I 'jibbed' like their

old cart-horse, and refused to stir a step in that direction. Then we talked about the different broods of chickens, and she showed me the hens that were good mothers, and told me the characters of all the poultry with the utmost good faith; and in all good faith I listened, for I believe there was a good deal of truth in all she said. And then we strolled on into the wood beyond the ash-meadow, and both of us sought for early primroses, and the fresh green crinkled leaves. She was not afraid of being alone with me after the first day. I never saw her so lovely, or so happy. I think she hardly knew why she was so happy all the time. I can see her now, standing under the budding branches of the grey trees, over which a tinge of green seemed to be deepening day after day, her sun-bonnet fallen back on her neck, her hands full of delicate wood-flowers, quite unconscious of my gaze, but intent on sweet mockery of some bird in neighbouring bush or tree. She had the art of warbling, and replying to the notes of different birds, and knew their song, their habits and ways, more accurately than any one else I ever knew. She had often done it at my request the spring before; but this year she really gurgled, and whistled, and warbled just as they did, out of the very fulness and joy of her heart. She was more than ever the very apple of her father's eye; her mother gave her both her own share of love, and that of the dead child who had died in infancy. I have heard cousin Holman murmur, after a long dreamy look at Phillis, and tell herself how like she was growing to Johnnie, and soothe herself with plaintive inarticulate sounds, and many gentle shakes of the head, for the aching sense of loss she would never get over in this world. The old servants about the place had the dumb loyal attachment to the child of the land, common to most agricultural labourers; not often stirred into activity or expression. My cousin Phillis was like a rose that had come to full bloom on the sunny side of a lonely house, sheltered from storms. I have read in some book of poetry,–

A maid whom there were none to praise, And very few to love.

And somehow those lines always reminded me of Phillis; yet they were not true of her either. I never heard her praised; and out of her own household there were very few to love her; but though no one spoke out their approbation, she always did right in her parents' eyes out of her natural simple goodness and wisdom. Holdsworth's name was never mentioned between us when we were alone; but I had sent on his letters to the minister, as I have said; and more than once he began to talk about our absent friend, when he was smoking his pipe after the day's work was done. Then Phillis hung her head a little over her work, and listened in silence.

'I miss him more than I thought for; no offence to you, Paul. I said once his company was like dram-drinking; that was before I knew him; and perhaps I spoke in a spirit of judgment. To some men's minds everything presents itself strongly, and they speak accordingly; and so did he. And I thought in my vanity of censorship that his were not true and sober words; they would not have been if I had used them, but they were so to a man of his class of perceptions. I thought of the measure with which I had been meting to him when Brother Robinson was here last Thursday, and told me that a poor little quotation I was making from the Georgics savoured of vain babbling and profane heathenism. He went so far as to say that by learning other languages than our own, we were flying in the face of the Lord's purpose when He had said, at the building of the Tower of Babel, that He would confound their languages so that they should not understand each other's speech. As Brother Robinson was to me, so was I to the quick wits, bright senses, and ready words of Holdsworth.'

The first little cloud upon my peace came in the shape of a letter from Canada, in which there were two or three sentences that troubled me more than they ought to have done, to judge merely from the words employed. It was this:—'I should feel dreary enough in this out-of-the-way place if it were not for a friendship I have formed with a French Canadian of the name of Ventadour. He and his family are a great resource to me in the long evenings. I never heard such delicious vocal music as the voices of these Ventadour boys and girls in their part songs; and the foreign element retained in their characters and manner of living reminds me of some of the happiest days of my life. Lucille, the second daughter, is curiously like Phillis Holman.' In vain I said to myself that it was probably this likeness that made him take pleasure in the society of the Ventadour family. In vain I told my anxious fancy that nothing could be more natural than this intimacy, and that there was no sign of its leading to any consequence that ought to disturb me. I had a presentiment, and I was disturbed; and I could not reason it away. I dare say my presentiment was rendered more persistent and keen by the doubts which would force themselves into my mind, as to whether I had done well in repeating Holdsworth's words to Phillis. Her state of vivid happiness this summer was markedly different to the peaceful serenity of former days. If in my thoughtfulness at noticing this I caught her eye, she blushed and sparkled all over, guessing that I was remembering our joint secret. Her eyes fell before mine, as if she could hardly bear me to see the revelation of their bright glances. And yet I considered again, and comforted myself by the reflection that, if this change had been anything more than my silly fancy, her father or her mother would have perceived it. But they went on in tranquil unconsciousness and undisturbed peace.

A change in my own life was quickly approaching. In the July of this year my occupation on the—railway and its branches came to an end. The lines were completed, and I was to leave —shire, to return to Birmingham, where there was a niche already provided for me in my father's prosperous business. But before I left the north it was an understood thing amongst us all that I was to go and pay a visit of some weeks at the Hope Farm. My father was as much pleased at this plan as I was; and the dear family of cousins often spoke of things to be done, and sights to be shown me, during this visit. My want of wisdom in having told 'that thing' (under such ambiguous words I concealed the injudicious confidence I had made to Phillis) was the only drawback to my anticipations of pleasure.

The ways of life were too simple at the Hope Farm for my coming to them to make the slightest disturbance. I knew my room, like a son of the house. I knew the regular course of their days, and that I was expected to fall into it, like one of the family. Deep summer peace brooded over the place; the warm golden air was filled with the murmur of insects near at hand, the more distant sound of voices out in the fields, the clear faraway rumble of carts over the stone-paved lanes miles away. The heat was too great for the birds to be singing; only now and then one might hear the wood-pigeons in the trees beyond the Ashfield. The cattle stood knee-deep in the pond, flicking their tails about to keep off the flies. The minister stood in the hay-field, without hat or cravat, coat or waistcoat, panting and smiling. Phillis had been leading the row of farm-servants, turning the swathes of fragrant hay with measured movement. She went to the end–to the hedge, and then, throwing down her rake, she came to me with her free sisterly welcome. 'Go, Paul!' said the minister. 'We need all hands to make use of the sunshine to-day. "Whatsoever thine hand findeth to do, do it with all thy might." It will be a healthy change of work for thee, lad; and I find best rest in change of work.' So off I went, a willing labourer, following Phillis's lead; it was the primitive distinction of rank; the boy who frightened the sparrows off the fruit was the last in our rear. We did not leave off till the red sun was gone down behind the fir-trees bordering the common. Then we went home to supper–prayers–to bed; some bird singing far into the night, as I heard it through my open window, and the poultry beginning their clatter and cackle in the earliest morning. I had carried what luggage I immediately needed with me from my lodgings and the rest was to be sent by the carrier. He brought it to the farm betimes that morning, and along with it he brought a letter or two that had arrived since I had left. I was talking to cousin Holman–about my mother's ways of making bread, I remember; cousin Holman was questioning me, and had got me far beyond my depth–in the house-place, when the letters were brought in by one of the men, and I had to pay the carrier for his trouble before I could look at them. A bill–a Canadian letter! What instinct made me so thankful that I was alone with my dear unobservant cousin? What made me hurry them away into my coat-pocket? I do not know. I felt strange and sick, and made irrelevant answers, I am afraid. Then I went to my room, ostensibly to carry up my boxes. I sate on the side of my bed and opened my letter from Holdsworth. It seemed to me as if I had read its contents before, and knew exactly what he had got to say. I knew he was going to be married to Lucille Ventadour; nay, that he was married; for this was the 5th of July, and he wrote word that his marriage was fixed to take place on the 29th of June. I knew all the reasons he gave, all the raptures he went into. I held the letter loosely in my hands, and looked into vacancy, yet I saw the chaffinch's nest on the lichen-covered trunk of an old apple-tree opposite my window, and saw the mother-bird come fluttering in to feed her brood,–and yet I did not see it, although it seemed to me afterwards as if I could have drawn every fibre, every feather. I was stirred up to action by the merry sound of voices and the clamp of rustic feet coming home for the mid-day meal. I knew I must go down to dinner; I knew, too, I must tell Phillis; for in his happy egotism, his new-fangled foppery, Holdsworth had put in a P.S., saying that he should send wedding-cards to me and some other Hornby and Eltham acquaintances, and 'to his kind friends at Hope Farm'. Phillis had faded away to one among several 'kind friends'. I don't know how I got through dinner that day. I remember forcing myself to eat, and talking hard; but I also recollect the wondering look in the minister's eyes. He was not one to think evil without cause; but many a one would have taken me for drunk. As soon as I decently could I left the table, saying I would go out for a walk. At first I must have tried to stun reflection by rapid walking, for I had lost myself on the high moorlands far beyond the familiar gorse-covered common, before I was obliged for very weariness to slacken my pace. I kept wishing–oh! how fervently wishing I had never committed that blunder; that the one little half-hour's indiscretion could be blotted out. Alternating with this was anger against Holdsworth; unjust enough, I dare say. I suppose I stayed in that solitary place for a good hour or more, and then I turned homewards, resolving to get over the telling Phillis at the first opportunity, but shrinking from the fulfilment of my resolution so much that when I came into the house and saw Phillis (doors and windows open wide in the sultry weather) alone in the kitchen, I became quite sick with apprehension. She was standing by the dresser, cutting up a great household loaf into hunches of bread for the hungry labourers who might come in any minute, for the heavy thunder-clouds were overspreading the sky. She looked round as she heard my step.

'You should have been in the field, helping with the hay,' said she, in her calm, pleasant voice. I had heard her as I came near the house softly chanting some hymn-tune, and the peacefulness of that seemed to be brooding over her now.

'Perhaps I should. It looks as if it was going to rain.

'Yes; there is thunder about. Mother has had to go to bed with one of her bad headaches. Now you are come in–

'Phillis,' said I, rushing at my subject and interrupting her, 'I went a long walk to think over a letter I had this morning–a letter from Canada. You don't know how it has grieved me. I held it out to her as I spoke. Her colour changed a little, but it was more the reflection of my face, I think, than because she formed any definite idea from my words. Still she did not take the letter. I had to bid her to read it, before she quite understood what I wished. She sate down rather suddenly as she received it into her hands; and, spreading it on the dresser before her, she rested her forehead on the palms of her hands, her arms supported on the table, her figure a little averted, and her countenance thus shaded. I looked out of the open window; my heart was very heavy. How peaceful it all seemed in the farmyard! Peace and plenty. How still and deep was the silence of the house! Tick-tick went the unseen clock on the wide staircase. I had heard the rustle once, when she turned over the page of thin paper. She must have read to the end. Yet she did not move, or say a word, or even sigh. I kept on looking out of the window, my hands in my pockets. I wonder how long that time really was? It seemed to me interminable–unbearable. At length I looked round at her. She must have felt my look, for she changed her attitude with a quick sharp movement, and caught my eyes.

'Don't look so sorry, Paul,' she said. 'Don't, please. I can't bear it. There is nothing to be sorry for. I think not, at least. You have not done wrong, at any rate.' I felt that I groaned, but I don't think she heard me. 'And he,–there's no wrong in his marrying, is there? I'm sure I hope he'll be happy. Oh! how I hope it!' These last words were like a wail; but I believe she was afraid of breaking down, for she changed the key in which she spoke, and hurried on.

'Lucille–that's our English Lucy, I suppose? Lucille Holdsworth! It's a pretty name; and I hope–I forget what I was going to say. Oh! it was this. Paul, I think we need never speak about this again; only remember you are not to be sorry. You have not done wrong; you have been very, very kind; and if I see you looking grieved I don't know what I might do;–I might breakdown, you know.' I think she was on the point of doing so then, but the dark storm came dashing down, and the thunder-cloud broke right above the house, as it seemed. Her mother, roused from sleep, called out for Phillis; the men and women from the hay-field came running into shelter, drenched through. The minister followed, smiling, and not unpleasantly excited by the war of elements; for, by dint of hard work through the long summer's day, the greater part of the hay was safely housed in the barn in the field. Once or twice in the succeeding bustle I came across Phillis, always busy, and, as it seemed to me, always doing the right thing. When I was alone in my own room at night I allowed myself to feel relieved; and to believe that the worst was over, and was not so very bad after all. But the succeeding days were very miserable. Sometimes I thought it must be my fancy that falsely represented Phillis to me as strangely changed, for surely, if this idea of mine was well-founded, her parents–her father and mother–her own flesh and blood–would have been the first to perceive it. Yet they went on in their household peace and content; if anything, a little more cheerfully than usual, for the 'harvest of the first-fruits', as the minister called it, had been more bounteous than usual, and there was plenty all around in which the humblest labourer was made to share. After the one thunderstorm, came one or two lovely serene summer days, during which the hay was all carried; and then succeeded long soft rains filling the ears of corn, and causing the mown grass to spring afresh. The minister allowed himself a few more hours of relaxation and home enjoyment than usual during this wet spell: hard earth-bound frost was his winter holiday; these wet days, after the hay harvest, his summer holiday. We sate with open windows, the fragrance and the freshness called out by the soft-falling rain filling the house-place; while the quiet ceaseless patter among the leaves outside ought to have had the same lulling effect as all other gentle perpetual sounds, such as mill-wheels and bubbling springs, have on the nerves of happy people. But two of us were not happy. I was sure enough of myself, for one. I was worse than sure,–I was wretchedly anxious about Phillis. Ever since that day of the thunderstorm there had been a new, sharp, discordant sound to me in her voice, a sort of jangle in her tone; and her restless eyes had no quietness in them; and her colour came and went without a cause that I could find out. The minister, happy in ignorance of what most concerned him, brought out his books; his learned volumes and classics. Whether he read and talked to Phillis, or to me, I do not know; but feeling by instinct that she was not, could not be, attending to the peaceful details, so strange and foreign to the turmoil in her heart, I forced myself to listen, and if possible to understand.

'Look here!' said the minister, tapping the old vellum-bound book he held; 'in the first Georgic he speaks of rolling and irrigation, a little further on he insists on choice of the best seed, and advises us to keep the drains clear. Again, no Scotch farmer could give shrewder advice than to cut light meadows while the dew is on, even though it involve night-work. It is all living truth in these days.' He began beating time with a ruler upon his knee, to some Latin lines he read aloud just then. I suppose the monotonous chant irritated Phillis to some irregular energy, for I remember the quick knotting and breaking of the thread with which she was sewing. I never hear that snap repeated now, without suspecting some sting or stab troubling the heart of the worker. Cousin Holman, at her peaceful knitting, noticed the reason why Phillis had so constantly to interrupt the progress of her seam.

'It is bad thread, I'm afraid,' she said, in a gentle sympathetic voice. But it was too much for Phillis.

'The thread is bad–everything is bad–I am so tired of it all!' And she put down her work, and hastily left the room. I do not suppose that in all her life Phillis had ever shown so much temper before. In many a family the tone, the manner, would not have been noticed; but here it fell with a sharp surprise upon the sweet, calm atmosphere of home. The minister put down ruler and book, and pushed his spectacles up to his forehead. The mother looked distressed for a moment, and then smoothed her features and said in an explanatory tone,–'It's the weather, I think. Some people feel it different to others. It always brings on a headache with me.' She got up to follow her daughter, but half-way to the door she thought better of it, and came back to her seat. Good mother! she hoped the better to conceal the unusual spirt of temper, by pretending not to take much notice of it. 'Go on, minister,' she said; 'it is very interesting what you are reading about, and when I don't quite understand it, I like the sound of your voice.' So he went on, but languidly and irregularly, and beat no more time with his ruler to any Latin lines. When the dusk came on, early that July night because of the cloudy sky, Phillis came softly back, making as though nothing had happened. She took up her work, but it was too dark to do many stitches; and she dropped it soon. Then I saw how her hand stole into her mother's, and how this latter fondled it with quiet little caresses, while the minister, as fully aware as I was of this tender pantomime, went on talking in a happier tone of voice about things as uninteresting to him, at the time, I very believe, as they were to me; and that is saying a good deal, and shows how much more real what was passing before him was, even to a farmer, than the agricultural customs of the ancients.

I remember one thing more,–an attack which Betty the servant made upon me one day as I came in through the kitchen where she was churning, and stopped to ask her for a drink of buttermilk.

'I say, cousin Paul,' (she had adopted the family habit of addressing me generally as cousin Paul, and always speaking of me in that form,) 'something's amiss with our Phillis, and I reckon you've a good guess what it is. She's not one to take up wi' such as you,' (not complimentary, but that Betty never was, even to those for whom she felt the highest respect,) 'but I'd as lief yon Holdsworth had never come near us. So there you've a bit o' my mind.' And a very unsatisfactory bit it was. I did not know what to answer to the glimpse at the real state of the case implied in the shrewd woman's speech; so I tried to put her off by assuming surprise at her first assertion.

'Amiss with Phillis! I should like to know why you think anything is wrong with her. She looks as blooming as any one can do.'

'Poor lad! you're but a big child after all; and you've likely never heared of a fever-flush. But you know better nor that, my fine fellow! so don't think for to put me off wi' blooms and blossoms and such-like talk. What makes her walk about for hours and hours o' nights when she used to be abed and asleep? I sleep next room to her, and hear her plain as can be. What makes her come in panting and ready to drop into that chair,'–nodding to one close to the door,– 'and it's "Oh! Betty, some water, please"? That's the way she comes in now, when she used to come back as fresh and bright as she went out. If yon friend o' yours has played her false, he's a deal for t' answer for; she's a lass who's as sweet and as sound as a nut, and the very apple of her father's eye, and of her mother's too' only wi' her she ranks second to th' minister. You'll have to look after yon chap, for I, for one, will stand no wrong to our Phillis.'

What was I to do, or to say? I wanted to justify Holdsworth, to keep Phillis's secret, and to pacify the woman all in the same breath. I did not take the best course, I'm afraid.

'I don't believe Holdsworth ever spoke a word of–of love to her in all his life. I'm sure he didn't.'

'Ay. Ay! but there's eyes, and there's hands, as well as tongues; and a man has two o' th' one and but one o' t'other.'

'And she's so young; do you suppose her parents would not have seen it?'

'Well! if you axe me that, I'll say out boldly, "No". They've called her "the child" so long–"the child" is always their name for her when they talk on her between themselves, as if never anybody else had a ewe-lamb before them–that she's grown up to be a woman under their very eyes, and they look on her still as if she were in her long clothes. And you ne'er heard on a man falling in love wi' a babby in long clothes!'

'No!' said I, half laughing. But she went on as grave as a judge.

'Ay! you see you'll laugh at the bare thought on it–and I'll be bound th' minister, though he's not a laughing man, would ha' sniggled at th' notion of falling in love wi' the child. Where's Holdsworth off to?'

'Canada,' said I, shortly.

'Canada here, Canada there,' she replied, testily. 'Tell me how far he's off, instead of giving me your gibberish. Is he a two days' journey away? or a three? or a week?'

'He's ever so far off–three weeks at the least,' cried I in despair. 'And he's either married, or just going to be. So there.' I expected a fresh burst of anger. But no; the matter was too serious. Betty sate down, and kept silence for a minute or two. She looked so miserable and downcast, that I could not help going on, and taking her a little into my confidence.

'It is quite true what I said. I know he never spoke a word to her. I think he liked her, but it's all over now. The best thing we can do–the best and kindest for her–and I know you love her, Betty–'

'I nursed her in my arms; I gave her little brother his last taste o' earthly food,' said Betty, putting her apron up to her eyes.

'Well! don't let us show her we guess that she is grieving; she'll get over it the sooner. Her father and mother don't even guess at it, and we must make as if we didn't. It's too late now to do anything else.'

'I'll never let on; I know nought. I've known true love mysel', in my day. But I wish he'd been farred before he ever came near this house, with his "Please Betty" this, and "Please Betty" that, and drinking up our new milk as if he'd been a cat. I hate such beguiling ways.'

I thought it was as well to let her exhaust herself in abusing the absent Holdsworth; if it was shabby and treacherous in me, I came in for my punishment directly.

'It's a caution to a man how he goes about beguiling. Some men do it as easy and innocent as cooing doves. Don't you be none of 'em, my lad. Not that you've got the gifts to do it, either; you're no great shakes to look at, neither for figure, nor yet for face, and it would need be a deaf adder to be taken in wi' your words, though there may be no great harm in em. A lad of nineteen or twenty is not flattered by such an out-spoken opinion even from the oldest and ugliest of her sex; and I was only too glad to change the subject by my repeated injunctions to keep Phillis's secret. The end of our conversation was this speech of hers,–

'You great gaupus, for all you're called cousin o' th' minister–many a one is cursed wi' fools for cousins–d'ye think I can't see sense except through your spectacles? I give you leave to cut out my tongue, and nail it up on th' barn-door for a caution to magpies, if I let out on that poor wench, either to herself, or any one that is hers, as the Bible says. Now you've heard me speak Scripture language, perhaps you'll be content, and leave me my kitchen to myself.'

During all these days, from the 5th of July to the 17th, I must have forgotten what Holdsworth had said about cards. And yet I think I could not have quite forgotten; but, once having told Phillis about his marriage, I must have looked upon the after consequence of cards as of no importance. At any rate they came upon me as a surprise at last. The penny-post reform, as people call it, had come into operation a short time before; but the never-ending stream of notes and letters which seem now to flow in upon most households had not yet begun its course; at least in those remote parts. There was a post-office at Hornby; and an old fellow, who stowed away the few letters in any or all his pockets, as it best suited him, was the letter-carrier to Heathbridge and the neighbourhood. I have often met him in the lanes thereabouts, and asked him for letters. Sometimes I have come upon him, sitting on the hedge-bank resting; and he has begged me to read him an address, too illegible for his spectacled eyes to decipher. When I used to inquire if he had anything for me, or for Holdsworth (he was not particular to whom he gave up the letters, so that he got rid of them somehow, and could set off homewards), he would say he thought that he had, for such was his invariable safe form of answer; and would fumble in breast-pockets, waistcoat-pockets, breeches-pockets, and, as a last resource, in coat-tail pockets; and at length try to comfort me, if I looked disappointed, by telling me, 'Hoo had missed this toime, but was sure to write to-morrow;' 'Hoo' representing an imaginary sweetheart.

Sometimes I had seen the minister bring home a letter which he had found lying for him at the little shop that was the post-office at Heathbridge, or from the grander establishment at Hornby. Once or twice Josiah, the carter, remembered that the old letter-carrier had trusted him with an epistle to 'Measter', as they had met in the lanes. I think it must have been about ten days after my arrival at the farm, and my talk to Phillis cutting bread-and-butter at the kitchen dresser, before the day on which the minister suddenly spoke at the dinner-table, and said,–

'By-the-by, I've got a letter in my pocket. Reach me my coat here, Phillis.' The weather was still sultry, and for coolness and ease the minister was sitting in his shirt-sleeves. 'I went to Heathbridge about the paper they had sent me, which spoils all the pens–and I called at the post-office, and found a letter for me, unpaid,–and they did not like to trust it to old Zekiel. Ay! here it is! Now we shall hear news of Holdsworth,–I thought I'd keep it till we were all together.' My heart

seemed to stop beating, and I hung my head over my plate, not daring
to look up. What would come of it now? What was Phillis doing? How
was she looking? A moment of suspense,–and then he spoke again.
'Why! what's this? Here are two visiting tickets with his name on, no
writing at all. No! it's not his name on both. MRS Holdsworth! The
young man has gone and got married.' I lifted my head at these words;
I could not help looking just for one instant at Phillis. It seemed to me
as if she had been keeping watch over my face and ways. Her face was
brilliantly flushed; her eyes were dry and glittering; but she did not
speak; her lips were set together almost as if she was pinching them
tight to prevent words or sounds coming out. Cousin Holman's face
expressed surprise and interest.

'Well!' said she, 'who'd ha' thought it! He's made quick work of his
wooing and wedding. I'm sure I wish him happy. Let me see'–counting
on her fingers,–'October, November, December, January, February,
March, April, May, June, July,–at least we're at the 28th,–it is nearly
ten months after all, and reckon a month each way off–'

'Did you know of this news before?' said the minister, turning sharp
round on me, surprised, I suppose, at my silence,–hardly suspicious, as
yet.

'I knew–I had heard–something. It is to a French Canadian young
lady,' I went on, forcing myself to talk. 'Her name is Ventadour.'

'Lucille Ventadour!' said Phillis, in a sharp voice, out of tune.

'Then you knew too!' exclaimed the minister. We both spoke at
once. I said, 'I heard of the probability of–and told Phillis.' She said,
'He is married to Lucille Ventadour, of French descent; one of a large
family near St. Meurice; am not I right?' I nodded 'Paul told me,–that
is all we know, is not it? Did you see the Howsons, father, in
Heathbridge?' and she forced herself to talk more than she had done for
several days, asking many questions, trying, as I could see, to keep the
conversation off the one raw surface, on which to touch was agony. I
had less self-command; but I followed her lead. I was not so much
absorbed in the conversation but what I could see that the minister was
puzzled and uneasy; though he seconded Phillis's efforts to prevent her
mother from recurring to the great piece of news, and uttering continual
exclamations of wonder and surprise. But with that one exception we

were all disturbed out of our natural equanimity, more or less. Every day, every hour, I was reproaching myself more and more for my blundering officiousness. If only I had held my foolish tongue for that one half-hour; if only I had not been in such impatient haste to do something to relieve pain! I could have knocked my stupid head against the wall in my remorse. Yet all I could do now was to second the brave girl in her efforts to conceal her disappointment and keep her maidenly secret. But I thought that dinner would never, never come to an end. I suffered for her, even more than for myself. Until now everything which I had heard spoken in that happy household were simple words of true meaning. If we bad aught to say, we said it; and if any one preferred silence, nay if all did so, there would have been no spasmodic, forced efforts to talk for the sake of talking, or to keep off intrusive thoughts or suspicions.

At length we got up from our places, and prepared to disperse; but two or three of us had lost our zest and interest in the daily labour. The minister stood looking out of the window in silence, and when he roused himself to go out to the fields where his labourers were working, it was with a sigh; and he tried to avert his troubled face as he passed us on his way to the door. When he had left us, I caught sight of Phillis's face, as, thinking herself unobserved, her countenance relaxed for a moment or two into sad, woeful weariness. She started into briskness again when her mother spoke, and hurried away to do some little errand at her bidding. When we two were alone, cousin Holman recurred to Holdsworth's marriage. She was one of those people who like to view an event from every side of probability, or even possibility; and she had been cut short from indulging herself in this way during dinner.

'To think of Mr Holdsworth's being married! I can't get over it, Paul. Not but what he was a very nice young man! I don't like her name, though; it sounds foreign. Say it again, my dear. I hope she'll know how to take care of him, English fashion. He is not strong, and if she does not see that his things are well aired, I should be afraid of the old cough'

'He always said he was stronger than he had ever been befc that fever.' 'He might think so, but I have my doubts. He w;

pleasant young man, but he did not stand nursing very well. He got tired of being coddled, as he called it. J hope they'll soon come back to England, and then he'll have a chance for his health. I wonder now, if she speaks English; but, to be sure, he can speak foreign tongues like anything, as I've heard the minister say.' And so we went on for some time, till she became drowsy over her knitting, on the sultry summer afternoon; and I stole away for a walk, for I wanted some solitude in which to think over things, and, alas! to blame myself with poignant stabs of remorse.

I lounged lazily as soon as I got to the wood. Here and there the bubbling, brawling brook circled round a great stone, or a root of an old tree, and made a pool; otherwise it coursed brightly over the gravel and stones. I stood by one of these for more than half an hour, or, indeed, longer, throwing bits of wood or pebbles into the water, and wondering what I could do to remedy the present state of things. Of course all my meditation was of no use; and at length the distant sound of the horn employed to tell the men far afield to leave off work, warned me that it was six o'clock, and time for me to go home. Then I caught wafts of the loud-voiced singing of the evening psalm. As I was crossing the Ashfield, I saw the minister at some distance talking to a man. I could not hear what they were saying, but I saw an impatient or dissentient (I could not tell which) gesture on the part of the former, who walked quickly away, and was apparently absorbed in his thoughts, for though be passed within twenty yards of me, as both our paths converged towards home, he took no notice of me. We passed the evening in a way which was even worse than dinner-time. The minister was silent, depressed, even irritable. Poor cousin Holman was utterly perplexed by this unusual frame of mind and temper in her husband; she was not well herself, and was suffering from the extreme and sultry heat, which made her less talkative than usual. Phillis, usually so reverently tender to her parents, so soft, so gentle, seemed now to take no notice of the unusual state of things, but talked to me–to any one, on indifferent subjects, regardless of her father's gravity, of her mother's piteous looks of bewilderment. But once my eyes fell upon her hands, concealed under the table, and I could see the passionate, convulsive manner in which she laced and interlaced her fingers perpetually, wringing them together from time to time, wringing till the compressed flesh became perfectly white. What could I do? I talked with her, as I saw she wished; her grey eyes had dark circles round them and a strange kind of dark light in them; her cheeks were flushed, but her lips were white and wan. I wondered that others did not read these signs as clearly as I did. But perhaps they did; I think, from what came afterwards, the minister did. Poor cousin Holman! she worshipped her husband; and the outward signs of his uneasiness were more patent to her simple heart than were her daughter's. After a while she could bear it no longer. She got up, and, softly laying her hand on his broad stooping shoulder, she said,–

'What is the matter, minister? Has anything gone wrong?'

He started as if from a dream. Phillis hung her head, and caught her breath in terror at the answer she feared. But he, looking round with a sweeping glance, turned his broad, wise face up to his anxious wife, and forced a smile, and took her hand in a reassuring manner.

'I am blaming myself, dear. I have been overcome with anger this afternoon. I scarcely knew what I was doing, but I turned away Timothy Cooper. He has killed the Ribstone pippin at the corner of the orchard; gone and piled the quicklime for the mortar for the new stable wall against the trunk of the tree–stupid fellow! killed the tree outright–and it loaded with apples!'

'And Ribstone pippins are so scarce,' said sympathetic cousin Holman.

'Ay! But Timothy is but a half-wit; and he has a wife and children. He had often put me to it sore, with his slothful ways, but I had laid it before the Lord, and striven to bear with him. But I will not stand it any longer, it's past my patience. And he has notice to find another place. Wife, we won't talk more about it.' He took her hand gently off his shoulder, touched it with his lips; but relapsed into a silence as profound, if not quite so morose in appearance, as before. I could not tell why, but this bit of talk between her father and mother seemed to take all the factitious spirits out of Phillis. She did not speak now, but looked out of the open casement at the calm large moon, slowly moving through the twilight sky. Once I thought her eyes were filling with tears; but, if so, she shook them off, and arose with alacrity when her mother, tired and dispirited, proposed to go to bed immediately after prayers. We all said good-night in our separate ways to the minister, who still sate at the table with the great Bible open before him, not much looking up at any of our salutations, but returning them kindly. But when I, last of all, was on the point of leaving the room, he said, still scarcely looking up,–

'Paul, you will oblige me by staying here a few minutes. I would fain have some talk with you.'

I knew what was coming, all in a moment. I carefully shut–to the door, put out my candle, and sate down to my fate. He seemed to find some difficulty in beginning, for, if I had not heard that he wanted to speak to me, I should never have guessed it, he seemed so much absorbed in reading a chapter to the end. Suddenly he lifted his head up and said,–

'It is about that friend of yours, Holdsworth! Paul, have you any reason for thinking he has played tricks upon Phillis?' I saw that his eyes were blazing with such a fire of anger at the bare idea, that I lost all my presence of mind, and only repeated,–

'Played tricks on Phillis!'

'Ay! you know what I mean: made love to her, courted her, made her think that he loved her, and then gone away and left her. Put it as you will, only give me an answer of some kind or another–a true answer, I mean–and don't repeat my words, Paul.'

He was shaking all over as he said this. I did not delay a moment in answering him,–

'I do not believe that Edward Holdsworth ever played tricks on Phillis, ever made love to her; he never, to my knowledge, made her believe that he loved her.'

I stopped; I wanted to nerve up my courage for a confession, yet I wished to save the secret of Phillis's love for Holdsworth as much as I could; that secret which she had so striven to keep sacred and safe; and I had need of some reflection before I went on with what I had to say.

He began again before I had quite arranged my manner of speech. It was almost as if to himself,–'She is my only child; my little daughter! She is hardly out of childhood; I have thought to gather her under my wings for years to come her mother and I would lay down our lives to keep her from harm and grief.' Then, raising his voice, and looking at me, he said, 'Something has gone wrong with the child; and it seemed to me to date from the time she heard of that marriage. It is hard to think that you may know more of her secret cares and sorrows than I do,–but perhaps you do, Paul, perhaps you do,–only, if it be not a sin, tell me what I can do to make her happy again; tell me.'

'It will not do much good, I am afraid,' said I, 'but I will own how wrong I did; I don't mean wrong in the way of sin, but in the way of judgment. Holdsworth told me just before he went that he loved Phillis, and hoped to make her his wife, and I told her.'

There! it was out; all my part in it, at least; and I set my lips tight together, and waited for the words to come. I did not see his face; I looked straight at the wall Opposite; but I heard him once begin to speak, and then turn over the leaves in the book before him. How awfully still that room was I The air outside, how still it was! The open windows let in no rustle of leaves, no twitter or movement of birds–no sound whatever. The clock on the stairs– the minister's hard breathing–was it to go on for ever? Impatient beyond bearing at the deep quiet, I spoke again,–

'I did it for the best, as I thought.'

The minister shut the book to hastily, and stood up. Then I saw how angry he was.

'For the best, do you say? It was best, was it, to go and tell a young girl what you never told a word of to her parents, who trusted you like a son of their own?'

He began walking about, up and down the room close under the open windows, churning up his bitter thoughts of me.

'To put such thoughts into the child's head,' continued he; 'to spoil her peaceful maidenhood with talk about another man's love; and such love, too,' he spoke scornfully now–a love that is ready for any young woman. Oh, the misery in my poor little daughter's face to-day at dinner–the misery, Paul! I thought you were one to be trusted–your father's son too, to go and put such thoughts into the child's mind; you two talking together about that man wishing to marry her.'

I could not help remembering the pinafore, the childish garment which Phillis wore so long, as if her parents were unaware of her progress towards womanhood. Just in the same way the minister spoke and thought of her now, as a child, whose innocent peace I had spoiled by vain and foolish talk. I knew that the truth was different, though I could hardly have told it now; but, indeed, I never thought of trying to tell; it was far from my mind to add one iota to the sorrow which I had caused. The minister went on walking, occasionally stopping to move things on the table, or articles of furniture, in a sharp, impatient, meaningless way, then he began again,–

'So young, so pure from the world! how could you go and talk to such a child, raising hopes, exciting feelings–all to end thus; and best so, even though I saw her poor piteous face look as it did. I can't forgive you, Paul; it was more than wrong–it was wicked–to go and repeat that man's words.'

His back was now to the door, and, in listening to his low angry tones, he did not hear it slowly open, nor did he see Phillis. standing just within the room, until he turned round; then he stood still. She must have been half undressed; but she had covered herself with a dark winter cloak, which fell in long folds to her white, naked, noiseless feet. Her face was strangely pale: her eyes heavy in the black circles round them. She came up to the table very slowly, and leant her hand upon it, saying mournfully,–

'Father, you must not blame Paul. I could not help hearing a great deal of what you were saying. He did tell me, and perhaps it would have been wiser not, dear Paul! But–oh, dear! oh, dear! I am so sick with shame! He told me out of his kind heart, because he saw–that I was so very unhappy at his going away. She hung her head, and leant more heavily than before on her supporting hand.

'I don't understand,' said her father; but he was beginning to understand. Phillis did not answer till he asked her again. I could have struck him now for his cruelty; but then I knew all.

'I loved him, father!' she said at length, raising her eyes to the minister's face. 'Had he ever spoken of love to you? Paul says not!'

'Never.' She let fall her eyes, and drooped more than ever. I almost thought she would fall.

'I could not have believed it,' said he, in a hard voice, yet sighing the moment he had spoken. A dead silence for a moment. 'Paul! I was unjust to you. You deserved blame, but not all that I said.' Then again a silence. I thought I saw Phillis's white lips moving, but it might have been the flickering of the candlelight–a moth had flown in through the open casement, and was fluttering round the flame; I might have saved it, but I did not care to do so, my heart was too full of other things. At any rate, no sound was heard for long endless minutes. Then he said,–'Phillis! did we not make you happy here? Have we not loved you enough?'

She did not seem to understand the drift of this question; she looked up as if bewildered, and her beautiful eyes dilated with a painful, tortured expression. He went on, without noticing the look on her face; he did not see it, I am sure.

'And yet you would have left us, left your home, left your father and your mother, and gone away with this stranger, wandering over the world.' He suffered, too; there were tones of pain in the voice in which he uttered this reproach. Probably the father and daughter were never so far apart in their lives, so unsympathetic. Yet some new terror came over her, and it was to him she turned for help. A shadow came over her face, and she tottered towards her father; falling down, her arms across his knees, and moaning out,–

'Father, my head! my head!' and then slipped through his quick-enfolding arms, and lay on the ground at his feet.

I shall never forget his sudden look of agony while I live; never! We raised her up; her colour had strangely darkened; she was insensible. I ran through the back-kitchen to the yard pump, and brought back water. The minister had her on his knees, her head against his breast, almost as though she were a sleeping child. He was trying to rise up with his poor precious burden, but the momentary terror had robbed the strong man of his strength, and he sank back in his chair with sobbing breath.

'She is not dead, Paul! is she?' he whispered, hoarse, as I came near him. I, too, could not speak, but I pointed to the quivering of the muscles round her mouth. Just then cousin Holman, attracted by some unwonted sound, came down. I remember I was surprised at the time at her presence of mind, she seemed to know so much better what to do than the minister, in the midst of the sick affright which blanched her countenance, and made her tremble all over. I think now that it was the recollection of what had gone before; the miserable thought that possibly his words had brought on this attack, whatever it might be, that so unmanned the minister. We carried her upstairs, and while the women were putting her to bed, still unconscious, still slightly convulsed, I slipped out, and saddled one of the horses, and rode as fast as the heavy-trotting beast could go, to Hornby, to find the doctor there, and bring him back. He was out, might be detained the whole night. I remember saying, 'God help us all!' as I sate on my horse, under the window, through which the apprentice's head had appeared to answer my furious tugs at the night-bell. He was a good-natured fellow. He said,–

'He may be home in half an hour, there's no knowing; but I daresay he will. I'll send him out to the Hope Farm directly he comes in. It's that good-looking young woman, Holman's daughter, that's ill, isn't it?'

'Yes.'

'It would be a pity if she was to go. She's an only child, isn't she? I'll get up, and smoke a pipe in the surgery, ready for the governor's coming home. I might go to sleep if I went to bed again.'

'Thank you, you're a good fellow!' and I rode back almost as quickly as I came. It was a brain fever. The doctor said so, when he came in the early summer morning. I believe we had come to know the nature of the illness in the night-watches that had gone before. As to hope of ultimate recovery, or even evil prophecy of the probable end, the cautious doctor would be entrapped into neither. He gave his directions, and promised to come again; so soon, that this one thing showed his opinion of the gravity of the case.

By God's mercy she recovered, but it was a long, weary time first. According to previously made plans, I was to have gone home at the beginning of August. But all such ideas were put aside now, without a word being spoken. I really think that I was necessary in the house, and especially necessary to the minister at this time; my father was the last man in the world, under such circumstances, to expect me home.

I say, I think I was necessary in the house. Every person (1 had almost said every creature, for all the dumb beasts seemed to know and love Phillis) about the place went grieving and sad, as though a cloud was over the sun. They did their work, each striving to steer clear of the temptation to eye-service, in fulfilment of the trust reposed in them by the minister. For the day after Phillis had been taken ill, he had called all the men employed on the farm into the empty barn; and there he had entreated their prayers for his only child; and then and there he had told them of his present incapacity for thought about any other thing in this world but his little daughter, lying nigh unto death, and he had asked them to go on with their daily labours as best they could, without his direction. So, as I say, these honest men did their work to the best of their ability, but they slouched along with sad and careful faces, coming one by one in the dim mornings to ask news of the sorrow that overshadowed the house; and receiving Betty's intelligence, always rather darkened by passing through her mind, with slow shakes of the head, and a dull wistfulness of sympathy. But, poor fellows, they were hardly fit to be trusted with hasty messages, and here my poor services came in. One time I was to ride hard to Sir William Bentinck's, and petition for ice out of his ice-house, to put on Phillis's head. Another it was to Eltham I must go, by train, horse, anyhow, and bid the doctor there come for a consultation, for fresh symptoms had appeared, which Mr Brown, of Hornby, considered unfavour able. Many an hour have I sate on the window-seat, half-way up the stairs, close by the old clock, listening in the hot stillness of the house for the sounds in the sick-room. The minister and I met often, but spoke together seldom. He looked so old–so old! He shared the nursing with his wife; the strength that was needed seemed to be given to them both in that day. They required no one else about their child. Every office about her was sacred to them; even Betty only went into the room for the most necessary purposes. Once I saw Phillis through the open door; her pretty golden hair had been cut off long before; her head was covered with wet cloths, and she was moving it backwards and forwards on the pillow, with weary, never-ending motion, her poor eyes shut, trying in the old accustomed way to croon out a hymn tune, but perpetually breaking it up into moans of pain. Her mother sate by her, tearless, changing the cloths upon her head with patient solicitude. I did not see the minister at first, but there he was in a dark corner, down upon his knees, his hands clasped together in passionate prayer. Then the door shut, and I saw no more. One day he was wanted; and I had to summon him. Brother Robinson and another minister, hearing of his 'trial', had come to see him. I told him this upon the stair-landing in a whisper. He was strangely troubled.

'They will want me to lay bare my heart. I cannot do it. Paul, stay with me. They mean well; but as for spiritual help at such a time–it is God only, God only, who can give it.

So I went in with him. They were two ministers from the neighbourhood; both older than Ebenezer Holman; but evidently inferior to him in education and worldly position. I thought they looked at me as if I were an intruder, but remembering the minister's words I held my ground, and took up one of poor Phillis's books (of which I could not read a word) to have an ostensible occupation. Presently I was asked to 'engage in prayer', and we all knelt down; Brother Robinson 'leading', and quoting largely as I remember from the Book of Job. He seemed to take for his text, if texts are ever taken for prayers,

'Behold thou hast instructed many; but now it is come upon thee, and thou faintest, it toucheth thee and thou art troubled.' When we others rose up, the minister continued for some minutes on his knees. Then he too got up, and stood facing us, for a moment, before we all sate down in conclave. After a pause Robinson began,–

'We grieve for you, Brother Holman, for your trouble is great. But we would fain have you remember you are as a light set on a hill; and the congregations are looking at you with watchful eyes. We have been talking as we came along on the two duties required of you in this strait; Brother Hodgson and me. And we have resolved to exhort you on these two points. First, God has given you the opportunity of showing forth an example of resignation.' Poor Mr Holman visibly winced at this word. I could fancy how he had tossed aside such brotherly preachings in his happier moments; but now his whole system was unstrung, and 'resignation' seemed a term which presupposed that the dreaded misery of losing Phillis was inevitable.

But good stupid Mr Robinson went on. 'We hear on all sides that there are scarce any hopes of your child's recovery; and it may be well to bring you to mind of Abraham; and how he was willing to kill his only child when the Lord commanded. Take example by him, Brother Holman. Let us hear you say, "The Lord giveth and the Lord taketh away. Blessed be the name of the Lord!"'

There was a pause of expectancy. I verily believe the minister tried to feel it; but he could not. Heart of flesh was too strong. Heart of stone he had not.

'I will say it to my God, when He gives me strength,–when the day comes,' he spoke at last.

The other two looked at each other, and shook their heads. I think the reluctance to answer as they wished was not quite unexpected. The minister went on 'There are vet' he said, as if to himself. 'God has given me a great heart for hoping, and I will not look forward beyond the hour.' Then turning more to them,–and speaking louder, he added: 'Brethren, God will strengthen me when the time comes, when such resignation as you speak of is needed. Till then I cannot feel it; and what I do not feel I will not express; using words as if they were a charm.' He was getting chafed, I could see. He had rather put them out by these speeches of his; but after a short time and some more shakes of the head, Robinson began again,–

'Secondly, we would have you listen to the voice of the rod, and ask yourself for what sins this trial has been laid upon you; whether you may not have been too much given up to your farm and your cattle; whether this world's learning has not puffed you up to vain conceit and neglect of the things of God; whether you have not made an idol of your daughter?'

'I cannot answer–I will not answer'.' exclaimed the minister. 'My sins I confess to God. But if they were scarlet (and they are so in His sight),' he added, humbly, 'I hold with Christ that afflictions are not sent by God in wrath as penalties for sin.'

'Is that orthodox, Brother Robinson?' asked the third minister, in a deferential tone of inquiry.

Despite the minister's injunction not to leave him, I thought matters were getting so serious that a little homely interruption would be more to the purpose than my continued presence, and I went round to the kitchen to ask for Betty's help.

''Od rot 'em!' said she; 'they're always a-coming at ill-convenient times; and they have such hearty appetites, they'll make nothing of what would have served master and you since our poor lass has been ill. I've but a bit of cold beef in th' house; but I'll do some ham and eggs, and that 'll rout 'em from worrying the minister. They're a deal quieter after they've had their victual. Last time as old Robinson came, he was very reprehensible upon master's learning, which he couldn't compass to save his life, so he needn't have been afeard of that temptation, and used words long enough to have knocked a body down; but after me and missus had given him his fill of victual, and he'd had some good ale and a pipe, he spoke just like any other man, and could crack a joke with me.'

Their visit was the only break in the long weary days and nights. I do not mean that no other inquiries were made. I believe that all the neighbours hung about the place daily till they could learn from some out-comer how Phillis Holman was. But they knew better than to come up to the house, for the August weather was so hot that every door and window was kept constantly open, and the least sound outside penetrated all through. I am sure the cocks and hens had a sad time of it; for Betty drove them all into an empty barn, and kept them fastened up in the dark for several days, with very little effect as regarded their crowing and clacking. At length came a sleep which was the crisis, and from which she wakened up with a new faint life. Her slumber had lasted many, many hours. We scarcely dared to breathe or move during the time; we had striven to hope so long, that we were sick at heart, and durst not trust in the favourable signs: the even breathing, the moistened skin, the slight return of delicate colour into the pale, wan lips. I recollect stealing out that evening in the dusk, and wandering down the grassy lane, under the shadow of the over-arching elms to the little bridge at the foot of the hill, where the lane to the Hope Farm joined another road to Hornby. On the low parapet of that bridge I found Timothy Cooper, the stupid, half-witted labourer, sitting, idly throwing bits of mortar into the brook below. He just looked up at me as I came near, but gave me no greeting either by word or gesture. He had generally made some sign' of recognition to me, but this time I thought he was sullen at being dismissed. Nevertheless I felt as if it would be a relief to talk a little to some one, and I sate down by him. While I was thinking how to begin, he yawned weariedly.

'You are tired, Tim?' said I.

'Ay,' said he. 'But I reckon I may go home now.' 'Have you been sitting here long?'

'Welly all day long. Leastways sin' seven i' th' morning.' 'Why, what in the world have you been doing?' 'Nought.'

'Why have you been sitting here, then?'

'T' keep carts off.' He was up now, stretching himself, and shaking his lubberly limbs.

'Carts! what carts?'

'Carts as might ha' wakened yon wench! It's Hornby market day. I reckon yo're no better nor a half-wit yoursel'.' He cocked his eye at me as if he were gauging my intellect.

'And have you been sitting here all day to keep the lane quiet?'

'Ay. I've nought else to do. Th' minister has turned me adrift. Have yo' heard how th' lass is faring to-night?'

'They hope she'll waken better for this long sleep. Good night to you, and God bless you, Timothy,' said I.

He scarcely took any notice of my words, as he lumbered across a Stile that led to his cottage. Presently I went home to the farm. Phillis had Stirred, had Spoken two or three faint words. Her mother was with her, dropping nourishment into her scarce conscious mouth. The rest of the household were summoned to evening prayer for the first time for many days. It was a return to the daily habits of happiness and health. But in these Silent days our very lives had been an unspoken prayer. Now we met In the house-place, and looked at each other with strange recognition of the thankfulness on all Our faces. We knelt down; we waited for the minister's voice. He did not begin as usual. He could not; he was choking. Presently we heard the strong man's sob. Then old John turned round on his knees, and said,–

'Minister, I reckon we have blessed the Lord wi' all our souls, though we've ne'er talked about it; and maybe He'll not need spoken words this night. God bless us all, and keep our Phillis safe from harm! Amen.' Old John's impromptu prayer was all we had that night.

'Our Phillis,' as he called her, grew better day by day from that time. Not quickly; I sometimes grew desponding, and feared that she would never be what she had been before; no more she has, in *some ways.

I seized an early opportunity to tell the minister about Timothy Cooper's unsolicited watch on the bridge during the long Summer's day.

'God forgive me!' said the minister. 'I have been too proud in my own conceit. The first steps I take out of this house shall be to Cooper's cottage.'

I need hardly say Timothy was reinstated in his place on the farm; and I have often since admired the patience with which his master tried to teach him how to do the easy work which was henceforward carefully adjusted to his capacity. Phillis was carried down-stairs, and lay for hour after hour quite silent on the great sofa, drawn up under the windows of the house-place. She seemed always the same, gentle, quiet, and sad. Her energy did not return with her bodily strength. It was sometimes pitiful to see her parents' vain endeavours to rouse her to interest. One day the minister brought her a set of blue ribbons, reminding her with a tender smile of a former conversation in which she had owned to a love of such feminine vanities. She spoke gratefully to him, but when he was gone she laid them on one side, and languidly shut her eyes. Another time I saw her mother bring her the Latin and Italian books that she had been so fond of before her illness–or, rather, before Holdsworth had gone away. That was worst of all. She turned her face to the wall, and cried as soon as her mother's back was turned. Betty was laying the cloth for the early dinner. Her sharp eyes saw the state of the case.

'Now, Phillis!' said she, coming up to the sofa; 'we ha' done a' we can for you, and th' doctors has done a' they can for you, and I think the Lord has done a' He can for you, and more than you deserve, too, if you don't do something for yourself. If I were you, I'd rise up and snuff the moon, sooner than break your father's and your mother's hearts wi' watching and waiting till it pleases you to fight your Own way back to cheerfulness. There, I never favoured long preachings, and I've said my say.'

A day or two after Phillis asked me, when we were alone, if I thought my father and mother would allow her to go and stay with them for a couple of months. She blushed a little as she faltered out her wish for change of thought and scene.

'Only for a short time, Paul. Then–we will go back to the peace of the old days. I know we shall; I can, and I will!'

Made in the USA
Middletown, DE
21 January 2016